Henry Reed's Big Show

HENRY REED'S BIG SHOW

By Keith Robertson

Illustrated by Robert McCloskey

A YEARLING BOOK

Published by
Dell Publishing Co., Inc.
1 Dag Hammarskjold Plaza
New York, New York 10017

For information address The Viking Press,
625 Madison Avenue, New York, New York 10022.

Yearling ® TM 913705, Dell Publishing Co., Inc.

ISBN: 0-440-43570-6

Reprinted by arrangement with The Viking Press.

Printed in the United States of America

Third Dell Printing—April 1980

CW

Henry Reed's Big Show

Friday, June 20th

Here I am in Grover's Corner again and it's good to be back. Grover's Corner is like a second home. Uncle Al and Aunt Mabel are always glad to see me. My dog Agony lives here all the time and he is glad to see me; and my friend Midge Glass lives in Grover's Corner and she is glad to see me too.

I'd better explain how I happen to spend my summers in Grover's Corner. My father is in the diplomatic service and he gets sent to posts all over the world. I've lived in Italy and England and South America and lots of other places. Traveling is fun, but moving every year or so gets tiresome. Several years ago Uncle Al and Aunt Mabel invited me to spend the summer with them because I'd spent less time in the United States than almost anywhere else. I've been coming back every summer since. Grover's Corner is

7

a quiet place. It isn't really a town, in fact there isn't even any corner here any more, just a blacktop road that goes through a cluster of ten houses out in the country, several miles from Princeton, New Jersey. There are woods and fields and open country, which makes it a wonderful place to spend the summer. There aren't many kids my age around but that hasn't mattered much because Midge Glass makes up for a half-dozen normal kids.

Midge Glass is my special friend and business partner. Her real name is Margaret but she's called Midge because she is so small. It's sort of odd to pick a girl as your best friend but I really didn't pick her. She was the only person, boy or girl, even near my age the first summer I spent here. She's a year or so younger than I am, but she's not the giggly type of girl, and she's much smarter than a lot of boys I know and more fun. We've been partners in a couple of businesses and she's always done her share of the work. It's not easy to find someone like that. You can depend on Midge.

I've kept a journal each summer but I wasn't going to keep one this year. However, since I went to the Music Circus last night I've changed my mind. If I'm going to be a theatrical producer, I should keep some sort of record. My friend, Mr. Seminoff, said it was a shame so few great producers and directors like himself didn't keep a day-to-day account of their early struggles and the decisions that shaped their careers. I expect I will have some struggles and I'll have to make some important decisions so I'll keep a journal after all. As Mr. Seminoff says, little things that don't seem important at all become important later when someone is trying to figure out how and why a man became famous. I asked Uncle Al if he would get me a notebook, and he brought one home last night.

"It's not a bad idea," he said when I told him I was going to keep a journal again. "Some pretty earthshaking things happen here in Grover's Corner when you and Midge get mixed up in some of your projects."

I arrived last Monday but nothing much happened until yesterday. I unpacked and strolled around Grover's Corner, getting used to it again, and of course I went to visit Midge. We talked over everything that had happened since last summer. Neither of us had any really good ideas about this summer except that we both want to do something that will earn some money. Tuesday evening, as we were eating dinner, Uncle Al asked me if I still planned to be a naturalist.

"I don't know," I said. "I'm thinking about becoming a stage director or producer."

"That's quite a switch," Uncle Al said. "What brought this on?"

"Mr. Seminoff, the famous producer and director, made a movie in the Philippines last fall," I explained. "We got to know him well and I visited the movie set and talked to him a lot."

"I see," said Uncle Al. "You got bitten by the movie bug and want to be a star."

"No, I don't want to act. I want to produce the show," I said.

"This Mr.—what was his name?" Uncle Al said.

"Seminoff."

"This Mr. Seminoff made quite an impression, I see," Uncle Al said. "I'm not up on who's who in the theatrical world and he may be a great new genius. If you want to produce and direct shows, more power to you. But knowing you fairly well and having known your mother *very* well, I'm going to make a prediction. I don't think you're going to find actors and actresses as interesting in the long run as bugs and worms and other animals. And maybe not as sensible either."

My mother is Uncle Al's sister, and they both grew up here in Grover's Corner. According to Uncle Al, she always had pigeons or turtles or rabbits or bees or some other animal, just as I usually do.

It isn't that I've lost interest in birds and animals and fish, but I'm not sure I want to make a career of being a naturalist. Producing a play or a movie is much more exciting. If I become a great producer and make a lot of money, I can still have all sorts of animals as a hobby. I could even have a little zoo of my own, which would be a lot of fun.

"I still like animals," I said. "Maybe I'll produce some animal shows too after I become famous."

"That's possible," Uncle Al said. "I'll make another prediction. If you become a producer, you'll be famous. The way things happen when you're around, it won't necessarily be the show that will make you famous, either." He gave several chuckles. "I'll bet any show you put on will be a lulu."

Uncle Al is no blood relation to my father but he talks more like him than like my mother. He says things that are hard to figure out and he laughs a lot when I can't see anything funny. Some people have a peculiar sense of humor. Uncle Al doesn't seem to be laughing at a person, though, or making fun of him. He sort of chuckles all to himself as though he has a private joke.

Wednesday evening at dinner, Uncle Al reached

in his pocket and produced four tickets. "They're to the Music Circus tomorrow," he said. "Since you've developed such an interest in the theater I thought it would be a good idea if we took you to one of our famous local entertainment spots."

"Where'd you get them?" Aunt Mabel asked.

"The Rotary Club bought out one whole section and is reselling them to make a little money," Uncle Al explained. "I got four because I thought your friend Midge might like to go."

"What is the Music Circus?" I asked.

"And what is playing?" Aunt Mabel wanted to know.

"In answer to the first question, the Music Circus puts on musical comedies during the summer. It is quite an unusual place over in Lambertville and I don't know how we missed taking you there before. I won't describe it but let you see for yourself. As for the show, it is a musical comedy called *The Girl From Prairie Junction*. I don't know a thing about it except that it is supposed to have some catchy numbers and is billed as a 'lighthearted comedy.' None of the shows at the Music Circus are new, Henry. They are all old favorites, ranging from Gilbert and Sullivan operettas to things like *South Pacific*."

"You'll enjoy it," Aunt Mabel promised.

She was right. I enjoyed it very much. Midge had been to the Music Circus before but I had never been to any place like it. The show is held in a great big tent like a circus tent and the decorations and refresh-

12

ment wagons and ticket office are fixed up like those of a circus. You have to drive down a long lane to get there and then you park your car in a field beside the tent. The inside of the tent is like a big bowl, with the seats sloping down toward the center. In the very center is the stage. People sit on all sides of the stage so there isn't any back the way there is in an ordinary theater. Because of this, you can't use painted backdrops or even furniture that is very high or someone wouldn't be able to see. Actually they didn't use very much scenery at all—just a few low benches or sofas or things like that. They also use trellises, arches, and doorways—things you can see through.

The actors get onto the stage by walking down the aisles and going up one or two steps. They can come from any direction, although most of them come from the aisle that leads down from the dressing rooms. At first it seemed peculiar for the actors and actresses to come walking down through the audience but after a few minutes you didn't notice it at all. You didn't notice that there was practically no scenery, either, but simply used your imagination.

The musical comedy was good. I liked the leading lady and man and both of them were good singers. In fact I liked everything until about the middle of the first act. Then a heavy woman with a huge mop of yellow hair came onstage. She played the part of the hero's mother and she didn't like the heroine in the play. I guess she didn't like her in real life either because she seemed to be trying to steal the show from

13

her. She hogged the center of the stage and somehow managed to get in the way so the heroine looked awkward. Of course she didn't look so graceful herself. She reminded me of a truck as she moved around the stage.

She was listed third in the cast of characters so I guess she had an important part. Her name was Lisa Analdi. I looked in the program and saw that she had about six songs that she sang alone. That was really bad news as far as I was concerned. I didn't like her or the way she sang. She sang one duet with her son in which she tried to drown him out. Her songs were supposed to be funny but she sang them as though they were "The Star-spangled Banner," with her voice quavering on the high notes. She threw her head back and sang to the top of the big tent instead of to the audience. I wasn't the only one who didn't like her. A boy behind me groaned each time she opened her mouth until I heard his mother tell him to behave.

"I think it's a case of mistaken identity," Uncle Al said at the end of the first act. "She thinks this is a Wagnerian tragedy."

I went to a Wagner opera one time with my mother and father. We were in Austria. I couldn't understand German and someone seemed to be dying every few minutes. It would have been better if this woman had been in one of Wagner's operas because she might have been one of those who died in the first act.

About halfway through the second act, the woman with the yellow hair started another of her solos. Just

14

as she hit a high note there was a mournful howl from somewhere offstage. I thought for a minute that some boy like the one behind me was making fun of her. I figured the noise wouldn't last long because someone would shut him up. But the howl continued. Then as Miss Analdi hit a high note the howl really hit its stride. I looked at Midge and she looked at me. We knew what had happened.

There was a short pause in the music and the singer lowered her head and looked into the audience to our right and frowned. She began singing again and the howl started again. Uncle Al leaned forward in his seat and looked past Aunt Mabel to where I was sitting.

"That sounds like a beagle, doesn't it, Henry?"

"A little," I admitted.

"Quite a little," Uncle Al said. "And like a beagle I know. Just where did you leave Agony?"

"In the car," I said. "I left the windows open a little but I didn't think wide enough that he could get out."

The woman hit another long high note and so did Agony. He was probably scared and lonesome, wondering where I was, and he didn't like the woman's singing any better than the rest of us. She had the advantage of the loudspeaker system but Agony gave her some real competition. He has a mournful howl when he is feeling sad and when that hit the tent top it bounced back and echoed all over the place. People started to laugh. Miss Analdi stood it for about two more bars and then she stopped, glared around the tent, and said, "I cannot sing until that noise stops!"

"I think maybe you ought to see if you can locate your dog," Uncle Al said. "I agree with Agony's judgment but his timing could have been better. She'll probably start all over now."

I got up from my seat and made my way past several people to the aisle. I looked around but I couldn't see Agony. After all, a beagle is pretty low to the ground and the tent was filled with people. He could have been anywhere. Judging from the howl, I thought he was off to my right, but sounds, especially inside a building or a tent, can be very tricky.

Then I saw a commotion three aisles over. About ten people got up from their seats and moved into the aisle. Several of them bent over as though they were trying to pick up something. They were probably trying to catch Agony by his collar. He's a very well-mannered little dog and anyone who knows him isn't afraid of being bitten. I guess Agony didn't want to be caught or maybe so many people all together scared him. I couldn't see him but he must have headed down the aisle toward the stage. One big, round-faced young man lumbered after him.

Suddenly Agony ran up on the stage. He went out to the middle and looked around. He didn't seem to be scared but just looking, probably for me. Someone began to clap. All at once the whole tent was filled with clapping and cheering. Agony was the star of the show.

Miss Analdi drew herself up as tall as she could, stuck her nose in the air, and looked at Agony as

though he smelled. I know he didn't, because I gave him a bath yesterday. She said something which I couldn't hear, but it wasn't very friendly. At this minute the big moon-faced man who was chasing Agony lumbered onto the stage and made a lunge for him. Of course he missed. I could have told him he was wasting his time. No slow-moving hulk like him could ever catch Agony. Agony just moved aside a few feet and kept looking around. The man made a second lunge and this time he hit one of the posts of a latticework affair that was supposed to represent a garden trellis. It came down just as the woman started to walk off the stage. Her head came poking through the top and the mop of yellow hair hung down over her right ear. It was a wig.

The trellis couldn't have hurt her very much when it fell because it was very flimsy. All the stage scenery is lightweight because people have to run down the aisles with it and put it in place. Miss Analdi let out a delayed shriek, pressed her hand to her heart, and looked as though she was about to faint. A man jumped up from the orchestra and someone else came onstage from the opposite side. They grabbed the trellis and lifted it up. The blond wig came with it. The singer's real hair was sort of brown and straggly but, at that, it looked better than the wig. She glared around a minute and then stalked offstage and up an aisle on the opposite side of the tent.

In the meantime, the big beefy man was still lunging around trying to catch Agony. I put my two fingers in my mouth and gave a shrill whistle. It took me a long time to learn how to whistle that way but it's worth it. When you want to whistle loud you can. Agony heard me. He stopped dead in his tracks and the man chasing him tripped over him and fell. He hurt Agony, who gave a yelp and then ran like a streak up the aisle toward me. I leaned down as he got near and he gave a jump. He landed right in my arms. I turned around and half-ran toward the rear, carrying Agony. He was licking my face and the crowd was cheering.

I took Agony back to the car and put him inside. Possibly he had squeezed through the space I left at the top of the window but I think someone opened the door by mistake and he jumped out. Anyhow, I rolled the windows up a little more, leaving only an inch at the top.

"Now you stay put," I told him. "You've caused enough trouble and the next time some big oaf might fall on you and mash you."

The show had started again by the time I got back. Another woman, much slimmer and much better, was singing the song. When she finished everyone in the tent clapped and cheered. The rest of the show was very good.

"I think it would be in order to locate the manager and say a few words of apology," Uncle Al said, as everyone started to file out of the tent.

I had been afraid he'd suggest that.

"What will I do if he wants me to pay for the scenery that was damaged?" I asked.

"I'll wait here," Uncle Al said. "It will be fifteen

minutes or so before we can get out of our parking place anyhow. I doubt if the damage is worth talking about, but if he brings it up, come get me and I'll take care of things."

Midge came with me. We asked some of the men taking the scenery off the stage where we could find the manager. One of them pointed to a tall, good-looking man at the top of one of the aisles that led to the dressing rooms.

"That's him, the man in the tan silk jacket talking to the two women."

We walked up the aisle and stood a few feet away, waiting for the manager to finish his conversation. After a minute or two he saw that we were waiting and turned toward us. I guess he was glad to get away from the ladies.

"What can I do for you two?" he asked pleasantly.

"I own the beagle that caused all the commotion," I said. "I'm sorry he broke up the show. I thought I had him safe in the car."

The manager grinned. He looked around carefully and motioned for us to follow him. We walked part way around the tent until we were away from everyone else.

"Don't give it a second thought," he said. "You did me a big favor. Miss Analdi quit, which is the best thing that could have happened. Probably saved the show. Her substitute is much better."

"I think so too," Midge said. "I liked the show."

"Good," he said. He reached in his pocket and produced two tickets. "Here are a couple of complimentary tickets for the show that starts next week. I think you will both like it. Your dog pulled the show out of the doldrums it was in tonight but I think next week it would be just as well to leave him at home."

"I will," I promised. "Thank you very much for the tickets."

We joined Uncle Al and Aunt Mabel at the entrance and started toward the car. "What did he say?" Aunt Mabel asked.

"He thanked us and gave us two free tickets for next week," I said.

Uncle Al has a funny habit of rubbing his hand over his lips and sort of blowing through his fingers. He did this and then said, "One time your mother got a birthday gift from our aunt. It was a fancy silk scarf as I recall, but she didn't like the color. So she took it back to the store to exchange it. She couldn't find anything she wanted and finally to get rid of her the store gave her money instead of the scarf. Now she had never been in this store before, but while she was there making a nuisance of herself she filled out a slip guessing how many buttons there were in a big jar in the window. A few days later she got a letter saying that she had won the contest and enclosing a check for ten dollars. These things probably run in a family, which proves that people don't always get what they deserve."

I didn't see any point to his story. "She guessed the closest, didn't she?"

"Yes," Uncle Al admitted.

"Then she deserved the ten-dollar prize."

"Funny," Uncle Al said. "Your mother said almost the same thing. To change the subject slightly, how do you feel about producing a show now that you've been to the Music Circus?"

"I'm really glad we went," I said. "It's going to be a lot easier than I thought."

"Easier?" Uncle Al asked. He turned around to look at me and almost went off the pavement in the process. Aunt Mabel doesn't do much back-seat driving, but she said she thought he'd better watch the road instead of me.

"Sure," I said. "I was worried about how I would get a theater with a stage and curtain and all that. But I could have a show right on our lot. Just build a stage and borrow some seats for people to sit on."

"How about the tent?" Uncle Al asked.

"I won't need a tent. I'm just going to put on the show once or twice. If it rains we can give people rain checks."

"I see," Uncle Al said. "I wasn't thinking about the physical problems of staging the show—just the personnel problems. As you saw tonight, actors and actresses can get temperamental. They sometimes try to hog the stage and they may walk off in a huff if they think they aren't treated right."

"I don't think there will be much problem that way," I said. "My cast is going to be kids about our age and they will be doing it just for fun."

"Maybe so," Uncle Al said. "But not too long ago I went to a Little League baseball game and things got hot and heavy between some of the players. You're going to have to be quite a diplomat to keep everyone happy. How are you going to get your cast, anyhow?"

"Well, I thought maybe Midge could help me," I said. "She knows every kid for miles around. We could have a party and invite all those she thinks might be interested."

"Would you get much of a turnout?" Aunt Mabel asked.

"If there was food," Midge said. "But I don't know how many would be interested in anything except the hamburgers and Cokes."

Midge hasn't been too enthusiastic about putting on a show but then I suppose that's because she's the practical type. It's really men who are the artists in the world—the great painters and writers, directors, and even chefs. I think she'll get more interested when we get started.

Saturday, June 21st

I went over to Midge's house today to talk about the party I want to have for the kids who might be in my theater group. We didn't get very far. In fact the whole day has been pretty much a waste of time as far as my show plans are concerned. I'd hardly walked in Midge's yard when she came rushing out the door.

"Hey, Henry, how would you like to go for a ride today?" she asked, all excited.

"Where to?" I asked, because I wasn't much interested in going to some place like a shopping center. My feet hurt whenever I get near a shopping center. Stores have the hardest floors in the world.

"Oh, just around," she said, waving her hand up at the hills. "On horses, I mean."

"Sounds all right," I said.

"Boy, you're enthusiastic!" Midge said.

Girls are funny about horses. When they become horse-crazy they really go off their rockers. I like horses and I like riding but there are other things that are just as much fun and maybe more. Girls who like horses are like women who coo over every baby they see. They think you're a traitor if you don't think every single one is wonderful. Anyone with any sense knows they aren't. Some babies are ugly and some horses are ornery and some of both are dumb. I could see that Midge was suffering from an attack of horse mania. She's very sensible ordinarily and we're old friends, so I decided to be nice and play along.

"Well, I haven't got any definite plans for today. A ride would be fun. What's the pitch?" I asked.

"The Gleasons have two horses and they're going away for the weekend. They'd like to have the horses get some exercise and we can ride them all day if we want."

I was about to say that I thought an all-day ride might be a little too much of a good thing but I didn't get a chance.

"We can make some sandwiches and take them along for lunch," Midge said. "There's some wild country over on Province Line Road. You can't get through with a car. We could eat our lunch someplace in the woods."

That sounded interesting so I agreed to go. Besides, I could see that Midge really wanted to, and you have to humor girls now and then. Also I wanted to stay on her good side because I'm going to need her help in my theater production. I went home and was back in about fifteen minutes with my sandwiches and a can of orange drink. Midge had a brown canvas knapsack like a flight bag and we put everything in that.

It turned out the Gleasons lived several miles away and Mrs. Glass drove us there. "Where are you going to ride?" she asked as we drove in the Gleasons' drive.

"Over toward Hopewell," Midge said.

"Will you be going by the Sillimans'?"

"Near there. We could go if you want us to. Why?"

"I owe Mrs. Silliman five dollars," Mrs. Glass said. "I was in the A & P last week and when I got to the checkout counter I found I didn't have enough money and I'd left my checkbook at home. Mrs. Silliman was in the next line and she lent me five dollars. I forgot all about it until just now."

"Give me the five dollars, and I'll deliver it if she's home," Midge said.

"Don't lose it," Mrs. Glass said. "And don't lose your way and stray into a frozen-custard stand and spend it."

"You're safe," said Midge. "I'm on a diet."

I don't know why Midge should be on a diet, because she is as thin as a toothpick. Midge has brown hair that is pulled back in a pony tail, blue eyes, and freckles all over her face. She's not as scrawny as when I first met her several years ago but she's still skinny. Anyhow, Mrs. Glass gave her the five dollars, let us out near the barn, and drove off. Midge started fussing with one pocket and then another, deciding where to put the five dollars.

"Why don't you let me carry that," I said. "I'm used to carrying money around and I've never lost any."

I was just trying to be helpful but she took it as an insult. "I am quite capable of holding onto five dollars for a few hours," she said. Girls are very sensitive if anyone suggests they can't do something as well as a boy. I don't know why. I wouldn't care if someone said Midge could sew better than me.

The horses were in their stalls, a big bay and a pinto. Both of them were well-fed and quiet looking. I've always been taught that you should be very careful around a horse, especially until you get to know it well. Maybe I was acting extra cautious as I led the bay, whose name was Ginger, out to the post where we were going to saddle them.

"Do you know how to ride?" Midge asked suddenly.

"Of course I know how to ride," I said. It was a silly question so I said, "I've ridden horses all over the world."

This was almost true. I rode several times when we lived in England and probably most often while we lived in Italy. And one time when we were in Sardinia I rode a donkey for an hour or so.

"These are both English saddles," Midge said. "No saddle horn."

"The saddle I used in England happened to be an

27

English saddle," I said, getting a little annoyed. I guess because I hadn't jumped up and down with joy when she suggested going for a ride, she thought I didn't know how to ride or was scared or something.

We cleaned the horses and saddled them and rode off. Ginger wasn't quite as quiet and well-behaved as I had thought. It wasn't that he did anything really bad but he would shy at all sorts of silly things, like a little piece of paper beside the road. I was carrying the knapsack with our lunch over my shoulder and each time we went faster than a walk, it would bounce up and down. This seemed to scare him so finally Midge took the lunch.

We rode along back roads for a mile or so until we came to a gate beside a small stream. There was a pasture on both sides of the stream with clumps of trees scattered around.

"This stretches all the way through to the next road," Midge said. "And there's a gate at the end. I've cut through here several times. It's fun riding along beside the stream."

I got off and opened the gate and then closed it after

we were through. Ginger was a big horse and getting back on him wasn't easy, especially as he wasn't too well trained and kept moving each time I got my foot in the stirrup. I had to make about six tries. I felt silly with Midge watching me suspiciously.

Part way through the pasture we came to a beautiful open stretch of smooth green grass. The horses wanted to run so we let them gallop for quite a distance. When we got to the other end of the pasture I got off again to open the gate onto the road. My comb dropped out of my pocket as I got off, and when I put it back I noticed that my glasses were gone. I wear glasses for reading but I don't need them all of the time. I knew I had put them in my pocket after I had finished saddling Ginger.

"I've lost my glasses someplace," I said.

"We can go back and look for them now or come back this way," Midge suggested.

"I think I'd better go back now," I said. "If I dropped them back on the road, some car might come along and run over them."

At first we were going to go back together and then we had a better idea. Midge went off to deliver the five dollars to the Sillimans. I went back to look for my glasses and we agreed to meet farther on up the road beside a high radio tower.

I rode along slowly, trying to retrace the way we had come. I hadn't gone any distance at all when I saw my brown leather glasses case lying on the grass. It must have bounced out of my pocket while we were galloping. I got off and picked it up, and this time I got back on Ginger on the first try. I gave a shout to Midge, thinking that I could catch up with her and we could ride over to the Sillimans' and back together. She didn't answer. I put Ginger into a gallop, thinking I would ride fast and catch her. We galloped a short distance and then Ginger dropped back to a trot and I changed my mind. My behind was getting a little tender. Somehow Ginger and I didn't seem to synchronize very well. Posting on a horse looks funny but it is the only comfortable way to ride at a trot. I had had a few lessons on how to post, but Ginger seemed to go up just when I wanted to go down and I bumped more than I posted. It doesn't take much of that when you haven't ridden for a long time to make you feel a little sore. So I decided to go on up the road at a nice gentle walk. I knew I would get to the radio tower long before Midge, but I could always get off and take it easy while I waited.

Ginger kept turning toward the stream and it didn't take much intelligence to figure out that he wanted a drink. I saw a nice shallow spot with a gravelly bottom so I rode him out into the middle of the stream and let up on the reins, and he promptly put his head down and began to drink. My shoestring had come untied so I leaned down to tie it while Ginger was busy drinking. That was a foolish thing to do. Something scared Ginger. I don't know whether it was a small fish, a falling leaf, or a bird flying by. It doesn't take much to scare him. I think he likes being scared. He jumped

31

about two feet to one side. I was already leaning way over and I wasn't expecting him to move. I pitched forward and landed face down in the stream.

The water was only about six inches deep and I didn't fall very far. But I banged my nose on a rock on the bottom and I was completely soaked from head to foot. I got to my feet, wiped the water out of my eyes, and looked for Ginger. He had forgotten all about whatever had scared him and was drinking again about three feet from me. I walked up to him and he made no effort to run away.

I led him out of the water and then paused on the bank to decide what to do. Water was dripping from my hair and clothes and squishing in my shoes as I walked. I looked down at my shirt pocket to see if I still had my glasses and saw that my whole shirt was covered with blood.

I put my hand up to my nose and, sure enough, I had a nosebleed. My nose bleeds very easily. All it needs is a little bump and it starts spurting like a fountain. Blood was running down with the water and dripping off my chin. I was wearing a new green-and-white checked sport shirt that Aunt Mabel had given me. If I didn't do something soon I could see it would be a red, green, and white sport shirt.

I was standing near a big clump of bushes and beyond them, back from the stream, was a small tree. I led Ginger over to the tree and tied him. Then I stripped off my shirt. My pants had blood on them too. The bushes hid me from the road so I took off my pants also. I took everything out of my pockets and waded out into the stream. Both my shirt and pants were made of these new materials that dry very fast and don't need to be pressed. I guess they don't stain very easily either, because the blood came right out. I pressed the water out of them as well as I could, and spread them out on a couple of the bushes where the wind and sun would catch them. It was a warm day with a good breeze and I knew they would be dry in a few minutes.

My nose was still bleeding and blood had run down all over my bare chest. There seems to be only one way I can ever stop a nosebleed, and that is to lie flat on my back and put my head way back. Usually I lie on the bed and let my head hang over the edge. I had to wait for my shirt and pants to get at least a little dry, so I picked a spot upstream where the bank beside the stream was high. I lay down on the grass on my back and let my head hang over the edge of the bank. I closed my eyes and relaxed in the warm sun.

It was nice lying there and I almost went to sleep. I had put my glasses, knife, handkerchief, and watch in a little pile a few feet away. Finally I reached out and looked at my watch and discovered that I had been there more than half an hour. I didn't know how long it might take Midge to get to the Sillimans' and back to the radio tower but I decided it was time to move. I felt my nose and it had stopped bleeding. I went down to the stream and carefully washed the blood off my face and chest.

My clothes looked much drier than they actually were. However, they weren't too bad, just sort of damp. My socks weren't too clammy but my shoes hadn't dried at all. About all you can say for them is that they didn't squish any more when I walked. If I hadn't expected to meet Midge in a few minutes I would have ridden in my socks and carried my shoes.

It took me only a minute to dress. I led Ginger the short distance to the gate, got on, and rode off down the road at a canter.

It was at least two miles to the radio tower and I kept Ginger at a canter most of the way. Between the sun and the wind I was practically bone-dry by the time we got there. I was drier than Ginger, who was beginning to work up a sweat. There was no sign of Midge so I led Ginger around a few minutes to cool him off and then tied him to a tree at the edge of the woods. I was sitting on a nice soft pile of leaves leaning back against a big tree when Midge arrived. She must have been making her horse move along too, because he was really wet.

"Find your glasses?" she asked.

"No trouble at all," I said, holding them up. "They bounced out of my pocket while we were galloping in that open stretch near the stream."

"Then you've been waiting for me for a long time," she said.

"Not so long," I said truthfully. "I fooled around at the stream for a while. Got my feet wet too."

"I'm sorry to be so late," she said. "But everything

delayed me. When I got there, Mrs. Silliman was on the telephone. I waited and I waited while she talked and she talked. Finally when she quit talking, I was able to give her the five dollars and get started. I decided to take the cross road instead of going back the same way. But they were repairing the road, and I couldn't get this idiot horse to go by that big roller. Maybe if I had insisted he might have but I decided the safest thing to do was go back. When I got down by the gate where we came out of that pasture, a car came whizzing up with a woman driving. Behind her was a state trooper in his car. They jumped out and ran through the gate. I decided to find out what all the excitement was about."

"What happened?" I asked.

"I still don't know," Midge said. "The woman claimed that someone had been murdered."

"Murdered? Where? Near where we were riding?"

"Someplace right beside the stream," Midge said. "It seems she is a bird watcher. She writes books and teaches classes about birds. Anyhow, she was walking along the top of that ridge looking for some kind of rare bird. She came from the same direction as we did. She was looking through her binoculars when she saw a nude corpse down near the stream. It was the body of a man and it was all mangled and horrible. The head was hanging over the bank and the face was covered with blood. She thinks his throat had been slit."

I kept a perfectly straight face. I suppose I should have told Midge what had happened but then I would have got involved in a long explanation. She would never have believed that I fell off Ginger while I was tying my shoelace. I could tell she didn't think I really knew how to ride and she would have thought Ginger had thrown me. If she was going to act so suspicious it would serve her right to wonder what had happened.

"Did you see this body?" I asked.

"No. We couldn't find it. The woman wasn't exactly certain where she had been, she was so excited. She had hurried all the way back to the other road—you know, where we came in. She had left her car there. She drove to the nearest house and called the police. When they came back they went into the pasture from this end so maybe that confused her. She claimed she knew roughly where she had seen him but there was no sign of anyone there. I rode up and down the stream for quite a distance and I couldn't see anything."

"Maybe she was imagining things," I suggested.

"That's what the state trooper suggested and she was furious. She was positive she had seen a bloody body."

"Maybe this body wasn't so dead," I said. "Maybe it got up and walked away. Did she feel its pulse?"

"She wasn't near enough," Midge said. "She said it was so bloody there wasn't any doubt about it. She saw it very clearly with her binoculars. Maybe whoever murdered the man came and took the body away." Midge looked around at the trees. "He could be someplace in the trees right now, burying the body."

"Maybe the wolves ate him," I said. "Which reminds me—let's have a sandwich."

"Disgusting!" Midge said. "How can you talk about wolves eating a bloody human body and then in the same breath ask for a sandwich?"

"I'm used to blood," I said, which is quite true because I've had a lot of nosebleeds. "Besides, my theory is that this woman made up the whole story and no one was killed at all. People will do anything for a little excitement."

Midge dismounted and got out the sandwiches. I noticed that the story about the dead man by the stream didn't seem to bother her appetite either.

"I have a feeling about this summer," Midge said as she finished her sandwich.

"What sort of a feeling?" I asked.

"That it's going to be an exciting one," Midge said. "In just a few days' time there was all that mix-up at the Music Circus and now there's this mysterious corpse that has disappeared. That vanishing body is some sort of sign. Don't you think so?"

My mouth was full so I just nodded in agreement.

"What do you suppose it's an omen of?" Midge asked. "What does it mean?"

I swallowed. "That things are not always what they seem," I said mysteriously. It was too late to tell her then. She never would have forgiven me.

Monday, June 23rd

I went down to inspect my barn this morning. Actually it isn't my barn but my mother's. My grandfather and grandmother once owned a big farm at Grover's Corner. They sold off some of the land along the road, which is where the five houses on this side of the road now are. They kept a lot of more than four acres and built a house on it. That's where my mother and Uncle Al lived when they were growing up. The house burned down a long time ago but the barn is still standing and in good shape. Midge and I used it for our research center the summer before last.

The barn stands near the front of the lot, about twenty feet from the road. There are solid trees across the back of the lot but most of the ground is open and covered with grass. There's a tree here and there. I suppose they were shade trees on the lawn of the house.

My grandfather and grandmother must have had a huge lawn. I'm glad I didn't have to mow it.

Going to the Music Circus was a big help. It certainly solved a lot of problems. I can put a stage about in the middle of the lot with chairs all around it. One little corner of the barn can be used as a ticket office and the rest of the barn as dressing rooms or storage space for what little scenery we need. You don't use much scenery when you have the stage in the center of the audience, which is a help. There is a second floor to the barn and I can make more dressing rooms up there if I need them.

The one important thing that the Music Circus has that I don't have is a great big tent. That helps when it rains but, as I said to Uncle Al, I will have to pick a night for my show when it doesn't rain. I will need a lot of chairs too. I can borrow quite a few right in Grover's Corner and if I can't get enough I can rent some. Uncle Al says you can rent folding chairs, usually from funeral homes.

I was walking around the lot, sort of imagining it all filled with people and my show about to begin, when I heard a whoop from across the street. Midge lives almost directly opposite my barn. She came screaming and shouting across the street at a dead run, acting like a lunatic. She rushed up to me, waving her arms and jumping up and down.

"The most wonderful thing in the world just happened to me," she said when she had calmed down a little.

"What?" I asked.

39

"Guess."

I hate this silly business of dragging something out by making the other person try to guess what you have in mind. "Somebody gave you a million," I said. "And if that isn't right I give up."

"Better than that," Midge said. "Somebody gave me a horse."

"A horse?" I said. "What kind of a horse?" This didn't seem like such wonderful news to me. In the first place I was still stiff and sore from our ride Saturday. I could hardly sit down on Sunday and some muscles that I didn't know I had still hurt when I walked.

"A riding horse," Midge said. "What did you think, a sawhorse?"

"That's wonderful," I said. I didn't really think it was so wonderful but there wasn't any doubt that she did. She was so pleased that she stood there staring off into space not seeing anything. I could tell she was thinking about all the fun she was going to have with a horse of her own.

"It's the most fantastic thing that's ever happened to me," Midge said. She flung her arms out wide and hugged herself. "Just think, me, Midge Glass, with a horse all my own. I'm so happy I could cry."

That's one of the things about girls I can never understand. They sometimes cry when they're happy. Of course now that I'm practically grown I don't cry at all if I can help it, but if I did it would be because I was sad or something hurt me. I started to sit down on a stump and then got up again. Sitting down has made me feel a little like crying ever since Saturday.

"Who gave you this horse?" I asked her.

"A business friend of my father's who's moving away," she said. "I think I'll call him Pegasus or Sir Launcelot." She looked off into space dreamily.

"When do you get Sir Launcelot?" I asked.

"Oh," she said, coming back to the world. "That depends on you."

"On me?" I asked. "What have I got to do with it?"

"Well, I have to have a place to keep him," she said. "I thought you might let me keep him in your barn. I'd let you ride him any time you want. He could sort of be your horse too while you're here during the summer."

Even though I was sore from riding, the idea of having a horse that was sort of half mine was interesting, and if I went riding fairly often I would get over being sore. Midge is my best friend and if she needed a place to keep her horse, I wanted to help her if I could. The only trouble was that I expected to use the barn for my theatrical production.

"I was planning on using the barn as a ticket office and for dressing rooms," I said. "I've decided to produce a show outdoors. Say, over there in the middle of the lot. I could put a stage there and chairs or bleachers all around."

"My horse wouldn't interfere with those plans at all," Midge said, full of enthusiasm. "We could build a stall at the back of the barn and the horse could go in through that door near the back. You could put several dressing rooms on this side of the stall and up on the second floor. I won't need any space for hay until late this fall."

"Actors and actresses are fussy," I said. "They might object to the smell."

"I expect to keep my horse and his stall very clean," Midge said stiffly. "Besides, several days before the show I could take him someplace else. Also, when you have your show you can use our garage and our playroom for part of the cast."

"Uncle Al has a good-sized tent that he uses to go camping," I said. "I could use that if I needed it."

"And we have a tent too," Midge said promptly.

"That would look good, add to the effect, having tents for dressing rooms," I said. "OK, it's a deal. You help me with my show and you can keep your horse in the barn as long as you like."

"Whoopee!" Midge shouted, jumping up and down. "I'm going to go call my dad. He's the only one left now to say yes. And since he found the horse in the first place, I know he'll agree."

She rushed back across the street to call her father and I went inside to look at the barn. As Midge had said, the horse could be kept at the back of the barn without interfering with the rest of the space. There was actually part of an old box stall left, and while the door leading outside had been nailed shut by someone, it didn't look as if it would be much trouble to open it. There was a trap door in the floor above and she could keep hay on the second floor and drop it down as she needed it.

Midge was back in a few minutes, all starry-eyed. "Guess what my father said?"

" 'Yes,' " I said.

"He said 'yes' and he said that over at the research center they took down quite a bit of post-and-rail fence which he can have. There's plenty to fence in all the open part of your lot, if you don't object to having a fence on your land. That would make a wonderful paddock for Launcelot."

Of course the lot isn't really mine at all but my mother's. Uncle Al takes care of it for her, although it doesn't need much care. Now and then the grass has to be cut but that is all. Uncle Al and Aunt Mabel are good friends of the Glasses' and I knew they would agree to Midge's keeping her horse there. I liked the idea of putting up a fence. We could put a gate near the barn. Then when I give my big show, people could buy their tickets, go past a ticket taker at the gate, and over to their seats. Without a fence around the area I would have trouble with people walking in without paying. Of course, anyone who really tried could sneak over or between the rails of a post-and-rail fence, but most adults won't climb a fence to keep from buying a ticket.

"Do you suppose there is enough fence to fence in all the lot back to the trees?" I asked. "If your horse ate the grass back there it would save mowing it."

"Perfect," Midge said, looking around the lot. "A private barn and his own pasture."

"What'll you do for water?" I asked.

"I'll carry it across the street," Midge said.

We went over to Midge's house and got some boards that were in back of her garage and a saw, a hammer, and a few other tools. By noon we had the box stall all repaired except for putting hinges on the door. We began working on a feedbox and manger. Midge must have spent quite a bit of time taking care of horses, because she knew exactly what she wanted. After lunch Mrs. Glass went to the hardware store for the hinges, and by five o'clock when Mr. Glass came home we had the stall practically finished.

"You did a fine job," he said. "If your horse isn't happy here he's crazy."

Mr. Glass helped us get the outside door unnailed. By dinnertime it was working again and ready to be used. The fence will arrive tomorrow and Mr. Glass has arranged for Mr. Baines, who owns the farm in back of the lot, to come with his tractor and dig the postholes. That will be a big help. I've helped Uncle Al dig a few postholes and that can be hard work. There's a lot of shale around here and the digging is terrible.

Thursday, June 26th

Well, I've had what you might call a theatrical production. Actually it was sort of an accident and I didn't really produce it but it has given me quite a bit of publicity. It was a lot of fun and everybody knows now that I'm in show business. I met some of Midge's friends who may act in my show. Also I learned that I'll have to get a permit to have a show. Especially with neighbors like the Apples.

I suppose I'd better start at the beginning and tell how it all happened. Tuesday morning Midge and I went over to the barn and started working again. Mr. Baines showed up about ten o'clock with his tractor and a posthole-digging attachment on the back. He gave us a lot of advice about the fence and helped us lay it out. Then he dug the holes. He would pull a lever on his tractor and a huge auger would drop down and begin turning. A posthole digger works just like a brace and bit does when it bores through wood. It was fun watching Mr. Baines work. He can really handle that tractor and drop the bit within an inch or so of the mark for the hole.

Mr. Baines finished at noon, and right after lunch a big truck arrived with posts and rails. The men unloaded them in a pile near the barn, and as soon as they had left, Midge and I started to work. Putting up a post-and-rail fence after the holes are dug is easy but it's a lot easier when you first start than after you've been doing it for several hours. We started at the back of the lot. Midge held the post straight while I shoveled some dirt around it. Then we tamped the dirt in tightly around the post, filling and tamping until we got the hole completely filled.

You not only have to keep the posts straight to make the fence look right, you have to keep the rails level. Midge and I put a couple of posts too deep and the rails zigzag up and down a little in a few spots, but the fence is good and strong and doesn't look bad. We got most of the back fence in and by that time we were so tired we quit.

After dinner Mrs. Glass and a friend took us to the Music Circus. Midge and I were able to use our two free tickets, which were for seats right at the front. It was a good show but nothing exciting happened as it had the first time.

We went back to work yesterday (that's Wednesday) right after breakfast. We discovered that Mr. Glass must have worked until dark while we were at the Music Circus. He had put in eight sections of fence, finishing up the back and part of one side. I was over being sore from my ride Saturday but now my arm muscles were sore from tamping dirt in postholes. I don't know how Midge felt. She's a lot smaller than I am but she carried posts and shoveled dirt right with me. Of course she was so anxious to get everything

fixed for her horse that she wouldn't have complained if she had been ready to drop.

By three in the afternoon, we had finished the front part of the paddock, the part that went parallel to the road. We left a space for a gate, which Midge said her father had promised to make. The front part ended at a corner of the barn. That left us only one side to do, and it was a short one. We were both tired and thirsty and I had two blisters on my right hand from tamping dirt. Midge went across the street and got us two Cokes. We sat down on the grass, leaned back against the fence, and rested.

"We need to paint out our sign," Midge said.

I had painted a sign on the end of the barn that said *Reed & Glass, Pure and Applied Research* back when we had had our research company. I'm pretty good at making signs, and even though the sign was faded, it looked all right. However, Midge was right. The sign didn't mean anything any more.

"We could call the place a ranch," I suggested. "That would sound very impressive—'Outdoor theatrical productions at the Bar Z Ranch,' or whatever we call it."

"Good idea," Midge agreed. "I'm all in favor of it. Only what will we pick as a name? Grover's Corner Ranch, Good Luck Ranch? It ought to be something catchy."

I suggested the Blistered Hand Ranch because of all the work we were doing on the fence or the Broken Glass Ranch because Midge was going to be broke when she had to buy feed for her horse. Midge didn't like either one or think they were funny at all. She came up with Sour Note Ranch, claiming I sing off key all the time, which I don't think is true. Finally we decided to call our place the R & G Ranch, for Reed and Glass. It may not be very clever but it is short and dignified.

"What will we do, paint right over the old sign?" Midge asked.

"We ought to paint the whole end of the barn," I said. "Uncle Al said it was about time to have the barn repainted."

"We could paint it if he'd get us the paint," Midge said. Midge may be small but she is not afraid of work.

The barn is red but it is beginning to peel in spots and looks sort of faded.

"Why don't we put up a temporary sign on a separate board?" Midge asked. "I have some heavy cardboard at my house."

I wasn't anxious to go back to tamping in fence posts so I agreed. We went across the street to Midge's house to get the cardboard. She had some pieces of white corrugated cardboard that had been part of a huge box in which their new refrigerator had arrived. We took two of them across to the barn. Midge got a marking pencil and in about five minutes I had sketched out a sign saying *The R & G Ranch*. I went home and got a hammer, some big-headed nails, and a stepladder. I tacked the sign up as high as I could reach on the end of the barn toward the road.

"Beautiful!" Midge said, standing back at the edge of the road. "That will make people sit up and take notice."

The sign wasn't beautiful, but I'm fairly good at lettering and at least I wasn't ashamed of it. Although I had used only one of the two pieces of cardboard, the sign looked huge. I guess it was the effect of the big spot of white against the red barn.

"I hope Trish rides by and sees that," Midge said. "Especially now that the fence is practically finished. You know, this place does look like a real ranch."

"Who is Trish?" I asked.

"Oh, an impossible stuck-up friend of mine," Midge said.

"If she's impossible and stuck-up, why is she a friend?" I asked.

"Well, she's not really so terrible," Midge said. "She has some good points. One of them is that she has a horse."

"I see," I said. "And you like to ride her horse?"

"No, but it's nice to have someone to ride with. You see, I've been able to use one of the Gleasons' horses a number of times but I haven't had anyone to ride with until you came. Trish doesn't live far from the Gleasons. Or rather her grandmother doesn't, and that's where her horse is. The grandmother is a big pain."

"In what way?" I asked.

"She gives Trish anything she wants. At least Trish claims that she does. The grandmother gave her the horse and just recently some very *fawncy* riding
50

clothes. The last time we went riding she looked at my blue jeans as though she didn't want to be seen with me." Midge looked down at her blue jeans. "I don't see anything wrong with these, do you?"

Her jeans were a faded blue-white and they had a few patches, but they looked fine to me. Lots of college students go to all sorts of trouble to get their blue jeans looking like Midge's.

"They look all right to me," I said. "Old enough to be comfortable."

"Trish isn't mean like the Sebastian twins were," Midge said. "She just gets on my nerves now and then. And she thinks she knows everything about horses."

"Speaking of the Sebastian twins, what's become of them?" I asked.

"They moved away," Midge said. "I guess they didn't buy the Apples' house at all but just rented it. Who do you think is living there now?"

"I can guess—the Apples are back."

"Right," Midge said. "They spent a year in California and hated it. Now they're back here hating New Jersey again. I hope my horse doesn't whinny a lot. They'll complain."

"They'll complain if he snores," I said.

The Apples own a big house next door to our lot. When Midge and I ran our research business in the barn, they were always complaining about something. Mr. Apple is a prim, fussy little man. Mrs. Apple is big, rather fat, and very excitable.

We went back to working on the fence but we were still tired. We were working halfheartedly on a post when a car pulling a house trailer came coughing and sputtering along the road. The car looked almost as bad as it sounded. Its fenders were dented and the paint was dull and chipped, with rusty spots here and there. The engine sounded to me as though it might quit at any minute. I guess it did to the driver, too, because he stopped in front of the lot, got out, and lifted up the hood. He was joined a minute later by two other men. All three stuck their heads under the hood and leaned over to look at the engine. From what little we could see of them, they seemed young—about twenty or so. The driver got back in the car and started the motor

again while the other two continued to look at the engine.

The motor started but it didn't sound any better. They tried various things but all it did was sputter and smoke. Then a fourth man appeared, although we wouldn't have been certain that it was a man if he hadn't been so tall. He was at least six feet four. Long black curls hung down to his shoulders. After he had looked under the hood for a minute he straightened and said something to the others. As he turned around we saw that he had a huge, bushy black beard. He glanced around and saw us.

He certainly looked like a giant as he came walking toward us. His shoulders were huge and his hands were the size of dinner plates.

"Our car seems to have fuel-pump trouble," he said when he got a few feet away. "Could we park our trailer off the road here for a while? I don't think we can pull it much farther. Without it the car might make it to a garage somewhere."

"Sure," I said. I pointed to the space we had left for the gate. "Can you back it in there?"

"Sure thing."

They unhooked the trailer from the car and the four of them pushed it around and through the gate onto the lot. They parked it a short distance from the barn and then asked us about service stations and garages. Midge knew more about this than I did. Finally the giant and one other man drove off, although the car sounded as though it would never get anywhere. One of the other two opened the trailer door and disappeared. A minute later he came back with a guitar. He sat down under the big oak tree beside the barn, leaned back against the tree, and began to strum his guitar. After a minute he began to sing. Midge and I listened for about fifteen seconds and quit work. He was good. He was singing a folk song about the hills of Vermont that I had never heard before. When he finished, both Midge and I clapped. He made a sort of mock bow.

"What are you putting up the fence for?" he asked.

"Midge is getting a horse," I said.

"That's wonderful," he said. "A horse is a noble

animal, and right now I wish we had one instead of a broken-down car."

He began strumming on his guitar and humming. Then after a minute he began to sing.

> "I'm just a poor stranded wayfarer
> In this lonesome lonesome land;
>
> I've traveled from Shanghai to Mayfair
> But I've walked as far as I can.

Oh, give me a horse, a noble horse,
    And I will ride him home. . . .
Won't somebody give me a horse?"

"Say, you're good!" Midge said.

"I think so too," he said. "The trouble is we're having some difficulty getting the rest of the world to admit it."

Just then the second man came out of the trailer carrying a trumpet. Midge looked at him and said, "Are you a group?"

"We are," said the man with the guitar. "We are the Willy Nillies, world renowned. Or we will be soon."

"We hope," added the young man with the trumpet. "I'm Pablo and the great lyricist with the guitar is Wong Lee."

"As you can see, Pablo is Spanish and I'm Chinese," said the guitar player.

Neither of them looked the slightest bit Spanish or Chinese to me but I guess these were their names in the group. Pablo put his trumpet up to his lips, leaned his head back, and began to play. Wong Lee began strumming his guitar and chanting some singsong words that sounded a little like Chinese but obviously made no sense at all. I'd never heard of the Willy Nillies and Midge said later that she hadn't either, but these two at least were wonderful.

They played for only a minute or two and then Pablo stopped, looked at his watch, and said, "You know, if they have to put a new fuel pump on that jalopy, they'll never get it fixed tonight."

56

"Then we'll have to stay here," Wong Lee said, shrugging his shoulders. He looked up at me. "Would it be all right with your parents if we camped here overnight?"

"I think so," I said. "They're in the Philippine Islands."

"Then our music won't keep them awake," Wong said.

"How about the rehearsal we were going to have?" Pablo asked.

"We'll do it here."

"Juice, man, juice," Pablo said. "We need juice for the amplifier. We can't get the sound effects Willy wants without it."

Midge nudged me and beckoned with her head. We walked over by the barn.

"I've got a wonderful idea!" she said. "Is there some way we can get electricity over here?"

"Well, if we had enough extension cords we could run power down from Uncle Al's house," I said. "The cords would have to cross the front yards of the two houses between."

"That's a long way," Midge objected. "My house is closer."

"We can't run a line across the road; the cars would run over it and ruin it," I said. "Maybe we could run it through that little culvert though."

"That would be perfect!" Midge said. "We'll find enough extension cords somewhere. Let's tell them we'll see that they have electricity if we can invite a few friends to hear them rehearse. We can get hold of kids who might like to be in your play. This will impress them."

It was a good idea and I told Midge so. We went back to the oak tree and spoke to Wong Lee.

"Sure, if we stay overnight. We like to have an audience. But until Willy and Vladimir get back I don't know what will happen."

About half an hour went by and then a car stopped in front of the lot and the giant and the fourth man got out. It turned out that the giant was Willy, the leader of the group. When Pablo explained the plan he was all in favor of it. In the meantime I had scouted around, and between the Glasses, Uncle Al, and the Ainsworths, I found enough heavy-duty extension cords to reach almost all the way from Midge's house to the barn.

We had a little bit of trouble getting the cord through the culvert. It's just a small culvert under the road, one of those corrugated pipes, and it was too small to crawl through. Finally I was able to push a rope halfway through with a long pole and then, with a hook on the end of the pole, fish it out from the other end. I tied the extension cord to the rope and pulled it through.

While I was hooking up the electricity, Midge was off telephoning some friends. She was still busy on the telephone when I heard Aunt Mabel ring the bell by the back step. I went home and ate dinner. I was at the table when Midge appeared. She had a big piece of cake in her hand, which she was eating. "I've got about seventeen or eighteen coming," she said. "With us we'll make quite a crowd. We ought to have Cokes or ginger ale."

"What's going on?" Uncle Al asked.

I explained what had happened. Uncle Al leaned back in his chair and grinned.

"I have to run into Princeton to mail a letter I want to go off first thing in the morning. I'll contribute a case of Cokes or whatever you decide you want. Only I want it understood that I want to be absolved of all responsibility in the matter."

"Gee, that would be wonderful!" Midge said. "Thanks."

Uncle Al usually has something in the back of his mind when he makes his mysterious remarks. I didn't understand that bit about no responsibility.

"Just what do you mean about being absolved of all responsibility?" I asked. "Is there going to be something wrong with these Cokes?"

"No. But I suspect that from just such a beginning as this, the famous Woodstock Music Festival started. I don't know whether you read about it, but it grew into a massive traffic jam that stretched back twenty miles."

I didn't see why he should be worried, since we couldn't have a traffic jam. The kids we invited weren't old enough to drive so their parents would bring them and go away again. What he said gave me an idea though. We still had the other piece of white cardboard. We could make a sign just for the evening and hang it up below the other one.

Midge and I hurried back to the barn. The Willy

Nillies had set up their amplifier outside the trailer but they were inside eating. Midge and I got the second piece of cardboard and made a sign:

Grover's Corner Music Festival
featuring
The Willy Nillies
Greatest Show since Woodstock

I was tacking it up on the barn when Wong Lee came over to see what I was doing.

"Very impressive," he said. "When we are world-famous, you can tell people that you sponsored one of our early outdoor shows."

I didn't tell him that I planned to be a producer. I don't doubt that they will become famous, but probably I will too. Maybe we'll meet again at some place like Lincoln Center in New York.

Midge's friends started arriving a few minutes after seven. At about seven fifteen Uncle Al showed up. He had not only a case of cold Cokes but one of ginger ale too. He stayed around a few minutes while the Willy Nillies got set up for their rehearsal. We connected the power to Midge's house and they plugged in their amplifier. More and more kids arrived by the minute. A lot of them must have invited friends, because there were some there that Midge claimed she hadn't called and didn't know.

Willy looked around at all the kids sitting on the grass and then turned to the other three. "We have
60

quite an audience, gang. I think you better get in uniform."

The three disappeared inside the trailer. I expected they would change into some sort of uniform or other, but when they came out a minute later you would never have recognized them. Wong Lee was wearing a long black wig with a pigtail like an old-fashioned Chinese coolie. Pablo had long straight dark hair that hung down to his shoulders and the fourth man, who called himself Vladimir, had sort of frizzy brown hair that just stuck out in all directions like a barberry bush. Of course Willy had had long curly black hair and a beard all the time. I suppose his hair was real, but I'm not certain.

"Ladies and gentlemen," Willy said in a deep voice. "Our latest number—'Never Mow the Lawn When It's Wet.' Lyrics by Wong Lee, music by accident."

They began to play. Vladimir played the drums, Wong his guitar, Pablo the trumpet, and Willy a piano accordian. Wong had told me earlier that Willy usually played a piano, but of course they didn't have one with them. Everyone in the group sang, but Willy and Wong were the only ones who sang solo. They were really good. They had a powerful amplifier and the music boomed out over the lot. After the first number, Wong turned it even higher and each time Vladimir hit the bass drum the whole barn shook. The audience loved it.

"Well, have a good time," Uncle Al said after the second number. "I think I'll mosey on home."

"They're terrific, aren't they?" Midge asked him.

"Terrific," Uncle Al agreed. "However, I'll be able to hear them all right at home. In fact I think all of Grover's Corner will be able to hear them all right."

About nine thirty Mr. Sylvester of the Princeton *Bugle* appeared. He was carrying his camera and a supply of flashbulbs.

"How do you suppose he heard about this?" I asked Midge.

"I called him," Midge said. "Free publicity. I think I'm going to be the publicity director for your theatrical company."

Mr. Sylvester has written several articles for his paper about Midge and me. I like him, but he always tries to write humorous stories about us and sometimes he half pokes fun at things that are serious, like the research business we had. I didn't want him making fun of my plans to produce a show. Adults sort of pooh-pooh young people's ideas at times. That's one thing I like about my Uncle Al. When I suggest I might do something, he listens, usually he grins, and then he says, "You'll never do it if you don't try."

I figured it was riskier not to talk to Mr. Sylvester than to talk to him, so I went over to where he stood. He had just taken a picture of the signs on the end of the barn.

"Quite an affair you've got going here," he said as I walked up. "This your idea?"

"Well, it was sort of an accident," I admitted. "They had trouble with their car and wanted to spend the night here. As long as they were going to do some rehearsing, Midge and I thought we might as well let people enjoy it. You see, later on this summer we're going to do a show here."

"What sort of show?"

"A play or a musical comedy," I said. "We're looking around for a good script now."

"You are, are you?" Mr. Sylvester said. "Now that's a coincidence. My niece, who is studying drama out at Iowa, sent me a play she wrote the other day. She wanted to know what I thought of it. Maybe you'd like to take a look at it. It appears you are closer to the theater than I am."

I told him that I'd like to see the play and he promised to drop it off at Uncle Al's office.

"This is sort of an impromptu music festival then," he said, nodding at Willy's group. "I don't believe I've heard of the Willy Nillies."

"They're fairly new," I said. "But I think they're going to be famous soon. Everybody here likes them."

That was true; all the kids who were sitting around listening thought the Willy Nillies were great. Only they didn't all sit around. Some of them were up dancing. Each time Willy's group stopped the kids all clapped and shouted for more. One of the things they liked was that Willie explained each number in advance and, with several songs he had just written, he would ask their opinions. He was interested and listened to what they had to say.

"Well, he does seem to be popular with this audience," Mr. Sylvester said. "And there's no doubt they're loud enough."

While they were taking a break between numbers, Mr. Sylvester went over and interviewed Willy. He took pictures of him, of each of the others, and then of the group together playing.

A few minutes after ten the Willy Nillies were in the middle of a very loud number when two cars drove up in front of the lot. I wouldn't have paid much attention if they had been ordinary cars but both of them had red lights flashing on top. Two state policemen and Mr. Allison, the township chief of police, came walking toward us.

"Who's in charge here?" Chief Allison asked.

"I am," I said. I didn't feel very good about admitting it but, after all, it was my lot and Midge and I had invited everybody.

"Well, we've had a complaint. In fact, several complaints. The principal beef seems to be that you are disturbing the peace with all the noise."

"Noise!" I said indignantly. "We aren't making any noise except when we clap. Everyody has been very quiet—just listening."

"I think people may have been referring to the band," Chief Allison said.

"That's music!" I said.

"Opinions seem to differ a little about that."

Just then Midge came hurrying over to where we were standing. She looked at one of the state troopers, a tall young man with a long narrow freckled face. "Hi!" she said. "How are you, Mr. Haywood?"

"Fine, Midge, how are you?" he asked.

"Henry, I want you to meet Officer Haywood. He

and I were on a murder case together. We were hunting for a mysterious bloody body that disappeared."

Officer Haywood shook hands with me.

"Did you ever find it?" I asked.

"No, I'm afraid I had to give up."

"What's the trouble?" Midge asked. "We aren't hiding any bodies here."

"We aren't looking for bodies tonight," Haywood said. "Just a little quiet. Some people say this is music, some call it noise, but it doesn't make much difference. A few people like to go to bed early and they are complaining that it's impossible to sleep. I think they may have a point. We stopped down the road about a mile and could hear your concert very plainly."

"The other complaint is that you are holding a concert without a permit," Chief Allison said. "Maybe you didn't know it, but you have to have a permit to hold any form of planned entertainment in the township—a concert, horse show, dog show—any affair that is open to the public."

By this time half the kids in the audience were gathered around us. They seemed to think it was wonderful fun and were making remarks about being raided by the police and asking if they were going to be hauled off to jail. I was the only one who felt things were serious.

"No one paid to come," I said to Chief Allison. "The Willy Nillies are rehearsing some of their new numbers and we invited our friends to listen. This isn't a planned entertainment—it's an accident."

"Well, we don't want to get accused of police bru-

tality by arresting everybody," Officer Haywood said. "But we think you better turn down the volume a little. Whether you are violating any township ordinances is Chief Allison's problem."

Chief Allison scratched his head. "Maybe there isn't any violation. I'm not sure. What I guess I'd better do is ask you to cut back on the volume a little, like Jim says. I'll make out a report and ask the township attorney for an opinion on whether you are violating the ordinance or not." He grinned a little. "That'll take a week or so, and by that time I suppose these young men will be gone."

"Who complained?" Midge asked. "The Apples, I bet."

"Well, I suppose you have a right to know," Chief Allison said. "It was Mr. Apple. You see, he's just beyond that hedge and I imagine this music shakes him up a little." He looked over at the group, who were singing and jumping around like wild men with their long hair flying all over. "I wonder how they get their hair combed out at night."

"They don't," I said. "Those are wigs."

One of the state troopers walked over to Willy at the end of the number and asked him to cut down on the volume. Then they all left. I saw Chief Allison's car stop a short distance down the road. He went in to see my Uncle Al. They're good friends.

The Willy Nillies played two more numbers and then said they were through. Everyone clapped and thanked them. Then we all went over to Midge's for some cake and to finish the rest of the soft drinks. The evening was a big success and Midge and I have quite a reputation already as producers of shows. I hadn't planned on this one at all, but now I can say I produced a rock show. The kids all say it was greater than Woodstock. Of course none of them went to Woodstock.

Uncle Al was sitting in the living room reading when I got home. "Well, how'd it go?" he asked.

"Great!" I said. "They were terrific, weren't they?"

"I would say sensational would be a good word to describe them," Uncle Al said, rubbing his chin. "And I don't think anything has created such a sensation in Grover's Corner since the day your mother opened the door to the dogcatcher's truck. Twenty-three dogs got loose."

"What did they do to her?" I asked.

"She claimed it was an accident," Uncle Al said with a funny smile. "And I dare say it was."

Uncle Al is always saying that I'm just like my mother, but then he'll tell a story about her which is interesting but doesn't seem to have any connection with the things I do at all.

Friday, June 27th

Midge has her horse. It wasn't easy and I've got my doubts about how things are going to work out, but the R & G Ranch is now in operation with a real live horse. Midge is so happy and puffed up with pride that she looks like a pouter pigeon.

Mr. Glass took the day off from work to go get the horse. Naturally Midge went along and she invited me. We left her house about eleven and drove to a big service station outside Trenton where they rent all sorts of trailers. They had camping trailers that fold out into tents, trailers for motor bikes, trailers to haul furniture, and two horse trailers. Mr. Glass picked the smaller of the two horse trailers and they attached a hitch to his bumper and off we went.

The people who gave Midge the horse are named

Wallach and they live about thirty miles from Grover's Corner. Midge had never seen the horse and didn't know much about it except what they had told her over the telephone. Actually they didn't give her the horse but just loaned it to her more or less permanently.

"Bernie Wallach is a mathematician," Mr. Glass explained. "He has been teaching at Rutgers, and he got an offer to go to England to teach for three years. So they're sort of giving Midge the horse while they're away."

"They'll probably never want him back," Midge said happily. "Mrs. Wallach said so. They are selling their farm, and when they do come back to the United States, they hope to be in California."

"Why didn't they sell the horse?" I asked.

"Because they're so fond of him," Midge said. "Mrs. Wallach says he's almost a member of the family."

I knew what she meant. I had a pet snake named Slimy one time that I felt was a member of our family. My mother liked him too, but as far as Dad was concerned, Slimy was an orphan. I had to get rid of him when we left Italy. I could have sold him but I didn't. You can't sell a friend. I gave him to a boy named Albert Gause whose father was in the Air Force and stationed in Italy. It didn't turn out very well because a month or so later Mrs. Gause shut the refrigerator door on Slimy and killed him. Knowing her, I'd bet she did it on purpose.

We stopped on the way to the Wallachs' and had a

sandwich. We arrived at the farm about one o'clock. Mr. Wallach was away somewhere but Mrs. Wallach came out to meet us. Mr. Glass introduced Midge and me to her.

"These two have really been working," Mr. Glass said. "They have a stall all ready and have built a post-and-rail fence enclosing about two acres of grass. I think your horse will be well cared for. The trouble is he may be spoiled."

"I wouldn't worry about that," Mrs. Wallach said. "Galileo is not easily spoiled. He has strong ideas of his own."

"Galileo?" Midge asked.

"That's his name," Mrs. Wallach said. "Bernie says he always has his eyes on the stars and that, among horses, he holds the same position Galileo did among mathematicians of his day in Italy. The name fits him perfectly and he is used to it."

There was no horse in sight but Mrs. Wallach walked over to the fence that surrounded a small pasture. "Galileo! Galileo!" she called.

About the fifth time she called there was a high-pitched whinny that sounded half like a laugh.

"There he is," Mrs. Wallach said. "He's hiding. It's a game he likes."

"How does a horse hide?" I asked. "They're sort of big for that, aren't they?"

"You don't know Galileo," said Mrs. Wallach. "I swear sometimes he can hide behind a car antenna. And there are other times I think he changes color like a chameleon and blends with the landscape."

Galileo would answer each time she called but he wouldn't come. The sound was quite near, so Midge and I climbed over the fence and began hunting. We found him in a clump of small trees not very far away. I don't know how we missed seeing his legs, because they must have been visible.

He didn't try to move or get away but just cocked his head to one side and looked at Midge as she snapped the lead on his halter. She led him out of the little clump of evergreens and started toward the gate. When you are leading a horse you can't really look at him. But I was walking behind and to the left and I could see Galileo all in one piece.

Without any question Galileo is the ugliest, awkwardest, most ungainly-looking horse I have ever seen. He is a buckskin, which is fine, because I like buckskins. Buckskins are sort of fawn-colored, and a good one usually has a dark-brown stripe running from his neck down his backbone to his tail. Galileo has this, but this is where all resemblance to ordinary horses stops. His head is too big, his neck is too long, and his whole frame seems to be sort of stuck together any old which way. He is loose-jointed and he slouches along, if a horse can slouch. Horses tend to put their ears back when they don't like something and forward when they're interested or curious. Galileo can't make up his mind which he is most of the time and has one ear forward and the other back. Now and then he reverses them.

His feet are much too big, and since they are hung on the ends of long, spindly legs, they look especially

73

peculiar. He shambles along as though each leg is proceeding independently. I watched his feet for a minute and wondered if he knew where he was going. I couldn't tell. One thing I did notice, though. He isn't as clumsy as he looks. There were rocks lying around in the pasture and somehow he managed to avoid them. He seemed to be sauntering along aimlessly, but he kept his nose right by Midge's ear. Every few feet he would reach out and touch her ear. He was fast, and by the time she turned around to see what had tickled her, he was looking off into the woods as though he didn't know she was there.

Even though Midge couldn't see Galileo as well as I could, she saw enough so that I knew she was a little upset. She was unusually quiet as she led him across the pasture. "He's very gentle," she said as Mrs. Wallach opened the gate.

"Oh, he's a lamb," said Mrs. Wallach. She put her arm around his neck and her cheek up against the side of Galileo's long head. He moved his jaw to one side, which gave him a funny lopsided appearance. He closed one eye and I swear he winked at Mr. Glass and me. I knew exactly what he was trying to say. It was, "She's out of her mind. I don't look a bit like a lamb and never did." Galileo was right. He doesn't resemble anything I ever saw before.

Among other things, Galileo looks skinny and underfed. His hip bones stick out, his legs are skinny, and his neck is sort of scrawny. But the grass was ankle deep in the pasture and there were delicious-looking patches of clover here and there. That is, they were delicious-looking to a horse, I suppose.

"What should I feed him?" Midge asked, looking at his hip bones.

"You can get a mixed horse feed at your local feed store," Mrs. Wallach said. "It will have oats, bran, a little corn, and some molasses. But we give him practically no grain during the summer when the pastures are lush." She must have seen Midge's glance at Galileo's skinny legs. "Don't let his appearance fool you. We worried about him when we first got him. We felt he should fill out and look nice and rounded the way some horses do, and we had the vet in to look at him several times. Then finally we figured out what was wrong. Galileo is smart, and eating all day the way most horses do just bores him. He has more important things to do than stuff himself with grass."

Midge managed to smile at this but I could see she wasn't too convinced. I had a vision of poor old Galileo having feed forced down his throat by Midge until he got fat.

Mr. Glass opened up the back of the horse trailer. The end gate is hinged at the bottom and folds down to make a ramp. Midge led Galileo over but he didn't pay much attention to her pulling on his lead rope. He walked along one side of the trailer, then around to the other, inspecting it. Then he went around to the back and walked right in.

"He likes to ride in a trailer," Mrs. Wallach explained. "We've spent part of each summer out at my parents' farm in central Pennsylvania and for several years we've taken Galileo along. There's a buggy out there and a harness. Galileo drives very well and we used to take long rides in the buggy. That's lots of fun."

Mr. Glass lifted up the tail gate and locked it in position by inserting two metal pins. Then we got the tack, which Mrs. Wallach was giving Midge along with the horse. There were two bridles, some extra bits, an extra halter, a Western saddle, and a saddle blanket. There were also some things like combs, currycombs, and brushes. We put the whole collection in the trunk of the car. The saddle was in good shape. Someone had rubbed a lot of saddle soap into the leather so it was nice and pliable. Mr. Glass and Midge thanked Mrs. Wallach again and we drove off. Midge was very quiet. I could tell she wasn't exactly delighted with the way Galileo looked.

"Well?" Mr. Glass asked after we had driven about a mile.

"She said he was very smart," Midge said. "But he doesn't look the way I hoped he would."

"Well, I'll admit he's not exactly a beauty," Mr. Glass agreed. "But there's an old saying: 'Never look a gift horse in the mouth.' "

"I've heard it but I don't know what it means," Midge said.

"Well, I suppose it refers to the horse's age," Mr. Glass said. "You look at a horse's mouth to find out how old it is. Whatever its age it's better than no horse at all. And I think you ought to feel that way about this horse. He isn't mean, she said he is reasonably well trained, he's smart, and above all he's yours for at least three years."

"Yes, I guess you're right," Midge said. "He's mine."

"Are you going to call him Launcelot?" I asked.

"Nope. He doesn't look like a Launcelot," Midge said. "He stays Galileo. Hey, look! Mrs. Wallach was right. He's enjoying the ride."

The horse trailer had a small square window in the front. It was a hot day and the window had been left open. Galileo had been tethered by his lead rope to a ring at the front of the trailer but it must have come undone because he was able to get his head high enough to poke his nose out the window. He was looking around at the scenery. His lips were apart and he seemed to be grinning.

I watched Galileo for a while but it wasn't easy from the front seat without getting a crick in your neck. Mr. Glass and I were in the front seat and Midge was in the back. She was rapidly getting over her disappointment in how Galileo looked and becoming more and more interested in him. She got up on her knees in the back seat and turned around to face out the rear window.

"I think he has a sense of humor," she announced without turning around.

"He probably does," Mr. Glass said. "You've heard of a horse laugh, haven't you?"

He winked at me and nodded back at Midge. She

was recovering. I figured if I wanted to make any remarks about Galileo I'd better make them, because she would soon be at the point where she'd get mad if you said anything that wasn't complimentary. As Mr. Glass had said, the horse had one strong point. He was hers.

We were driving slowly because Mr. Glass said if we went much faster than thirty-five miles an hour the trailer began to sway and the car was difficult to manage. Cars kept honking at us so when we got near home, where Mr. Glass knew all the back roads, we left the main highway. We were about four miles from Grover's Corner when we came to a long hill known as Murphy's Slope. I had been there several times before and I remembered Midge pointing out how long the hill is. There isn't much traffic on the road and in winter they sometimes block off the hill and the kids all go sledding. Of course I never have because I've never been in Grover's Corner in the winter but Midge said she had. The road curves about halfway down, and if you don't turn your sled with it, you go off a bank into the woods. You do with a car too so Mr. Glass went even slower.

We were about a third of the way down the hill when Midge gave a shriek. "The trailer is loose!"

Mr. Glass started to turn and then jerked his eyes back to the road. He glanced up at the rear-view mirror. I half turned around in the seat and got up on one knee. Sure enough, the trailer wasn't attached to the car any more. It was bumping along behind us about twenty feet back.

78

"It's rolling downhill all by itself!" Midge shouted. "And the tongue keeps bumping on the road. Poor Galileo! He's going to be all shook up!"

"Don't scream so," Mr. Glass said. "I'm trying to think of something to do."

He put on the brakes very lightly and we slowed.

"It's gaining on us. It's going to bump into us!" Midge shouted.

"That's what I hope," Mr. Glass said. "It's the only way I know to stop it. If it doesn't bang too hard, he'll probably be all right."

None of us said anything for several seconds that seemed like weeks. Then suddenly when the trailer was only a few feet behind us, it swerved to the left side of the road. Before we knew what was happening it was right up even with us and still going. Galileo stuck his head out the little square window, and I swear he was laughing. He was enjoying the ride and I guess he thought he was very smart passing us that way.

Mr. Glass glanced at the trailer and then back at the road. He didn't know what to do and neither did Midge or I. We were still slowing while the trailer was picking up speed very rapidly. It got a few feet ahead of us and then suddenly swerved back from the left side of the road to the right. It was going faster and faster all the time. The tongue, which was banging and bumping on the macadam road, might gouge into something any second. That would bring the trailer to a sudden halt and we would plow into it. Mr. Glass did the only thing he could—he jammed on the brakes and let the trailer go racing on ahead of us. We came almost to a stop. The trailer reached the curve and instead of plunging off the bank as I expected, it swerved. It had been gyrating back and forth across the road and something made it swerve to the left at just the right time. A moment later it had disappeared.

"He'll be killed!" Midge moaned. "Poor Galileo! And I never even got to ride him."

Mr. Glass took a handkerchief from his pocket and wiped his forehead.

"Can't we go any faster?" Midge asked. "We've got to catch him."

"If we are a minute or two late in catching up to the trailer it won't make any difference to Galileo at this point," Mr. Glass said. "That trailer is not going to stop until it bumps into something solid. And I need a few seconds to steady my nerves."

He put his handkerchief away and we picked up speed again. We rounded the curve and could see the bottom of the hill, but there was no trailer in sight.

"It may have gone off either side into the woods," Mr. Glass said. "I'll watch the left side and you watch the right, Henry." Midge was too excited to watch anything carefully.

Near the bottom of the hill, Mr. Glass spotted the trailer. It had gone off the road on the left, snapped a barbed-wire fence, and rolled over a big clump of witch hazel. You could just see the top of the trailer over the half-mashed bush. Mr. Glass pulled the car off onto the shoulder of the road and we all climbed out. Midge was out first. She ran across the road, down the little sloping bank, and into the woods.

"He's disappeared!" she shouted. "He must have bounced out on the way down!"

"How could he bounce out?" Mr. Glass asked. "Don't be silly."

We went around the bush to look at the trailer. The nice new red paint had been scratched and the tongue had been bent a little, but it didn't look to be in bad shape. The two pins which slid through the holes to fasten the end gate were gone and it was open.

"He's dead! I know he's dead!" Midge wailed.

"Quit the caterwauling," Mr. Glass said. He looked at the ground and drew a deep breath of relief. "He's not dead. He's certainly not a zombie, and he walked away from here. Look!"

We looked where he was pointing and there were hoof marks. Galileo had backed out of the trailer and had gone off somewhere. I didn't blame him. After that hair-raising ride, I wouldn't stick around either.

"He may be shaken up a little," I said. "But he's able to walk."

"I guess the first thing to do is to find him," Mr.

Glass said. "You two start hunting. I'll see if I can figure out how to get this trailer back on the road."

The ground around the trailer seemed to be the only soft spot in the area, because after the first few feet, I couldn't find any more tracks. There was nothing to do but wander around through the trees looking for him. We looked for at least ten minutes without finding a sign of him.

"Maybe he went back to the road and hitched a ride with someone else," I suggested to Midge.

"It isn't funny," she said. "He may be bleeding to death someplace. I wonder if horses go off to a secluded place to die, like elephants."

Mr. Glass called to me and I hurried back. He had managed to get the trailer turned around, but pulling it through those woods over the bumpy ground was more than he could manage. He had hooked two of the lead ropes and a piece of chain to form a tow rope and had backed the car around. We fastened the rope to the bumper hitch and I guided the trailer while he drove the car. Finally we managed to pull the trailer back onto the road. Although the tongue was bent, the hitch was still usable. In a few minutes we had the trailer hooked to the car once more.

I looked inside. The lead rope which had been attached to Galileo's halter wasn't broken. It was simply gone.

"His lead rope must have come untied," I told Mr. Glass. "At least we'll have something we can grab when we do find him."

"I don't see how it could have come untied," Mr.

Glass said. "I tied that myself and was very careful about it. However, if it did, it did."

The three of us began hunting for Galileo, going in bigger and bigger circles around the spot where the trailer had stopped. Finally Mr. Glass called a conference.

"Maybe Mrs. Wallach was right about that horse," he said when we had all gathered together back near the road. "Maybe he didn't wander off but is hiding. If he wants to play games, we'll have to play. Midge, you can come the closest to imitating Mrs. Wallach's voice. You call him. Henry and I will cruise around and listen."

Mr. Glass went into the woods at least five or six hundred feet but I stayed close to the road. Midge stood on the shoulder of the highway and called "Galileo! Galileo! Where are you, Galileo?" She did a good job of making her voice deep. She sounded very much like Mrs. Wallach. About the fourth time she called I heard a whinny so close that I jumped. I looked around and the only possible place for him to be was a clump of four or five cedars. I started toward them when I heard a yowl of pain from Midge. Midge is small, but she can really turn on the volume when she wants to.

"What's the matter?" I shouted.

The only answer I got was some more moaning and groaning. I glanced at the clump of trees and decided Galileo would probably wait. I hurried toward the road. Midge was sitting on the ground at the bottom of the shoulder, rocking back and forth and holding her knee. There wasn't any need to ask what had hap-

84

pened. She had heard the whinny too and probably had started running toward it. She had tripped and gouged her knee on what later turned out to be part of a broken bottle some litterbug had thrown out beside the highway. She was wearing shorts, so her knees had no protection at all. She must have given herself quite a bad cut because her leg was already covered with blood.

Mr. Glass arrived a few seconds after I did and took charge. He had a first-aid kit in the back of the car, so while he fixed Midge's knee, I went back to where I thought Galileo was hiding. I had been by that clump of trees three or four times and I knew it wasn't big enough or thick enough for a horse to be hiding in the middle of it. I bent over so that I could watch the ground as I walked around. Galileo was walking on the other side, moving just fast enough to keep the trees between us. I stopped and he stopped.

The trees were almost touching each other, but by holding the branches back you could squeeze through. I pushed through the middle and came out the other side. Galileo stood perfectly still while I grabbed his lead rope. He'd had his fun, I guess, and didn't care whether he was caught or not. I called to Midge and Mr. Glass, and headed back to the road.

We looked Galileo over carefully and couldn't find a scratch. The trailer must not have stopped too suddenly. Of course he might have a few bruises, but he doesn't limp at all.

"Poor horse," Midge said, limping over to pat his neck. "Poor Galileo. Were you scared?"

"He wasn't half as scared as I was," Mr. Glass said. "I'm the one who deserves the sympathy."

Although the trailer looked all right, Mr. Glass said he would rather not put Galileo back in it. There must have been something wrong with the hitch in the first place or it never would have come uncoupled.

"It's only about four miles," he said. "I think the safest thing to do is to saddle him and ride him the rest of the way."

Midge was in no condition to ride with a bum knee. There wasn't much I could do but volunteer. I had just got over feeling sore from my last ride and I wasn't anxious to take another. Girls are always talking about the advantages of being a man, but there are disadvantages too. You are expected to carry heavy suitcases and ride strange horses home and all sorts of things. But of course I said I'd be glad to ride Galileo.

We saddled him and I got on. Galileo was very well-behaved, and that ambling, shambling walk of his is very comfortable. Mr. Glass and Midge trailed along behind in the car for at least half a mile to make certain that I didn't have any trouble. Then I told them I was sure he would behave, so they drove on.

Half of Grover's Corner turned out to see Midge's horse arrive. Even Mrs. Apple stood on the corner of her lot and watched. She looked very grouchy and disapproving as I rode by but I didn't pay any attention. Uncle Al had checked the zoning regulations. Grover's Corner is unincorporated and classified rural. It's legal to have a horse here.

Everyone was very polite as I rode through the gate into the corral. But I didn't hear anyone say, "What a beautiful horse!" Agony was the most enthusiastic of all the spectators. He scampered around and barked at the top of his voice. I could tell he liked Galileo.

I was wearing a flat-topped straw hat with a green ribbon around the crown. I had bought it a few days before, and I liked it because it was cool, kept the sun out of my eyes, and looked sharp. As I got off Galileo, he reached out and took a huge bite out of the brim. The straw was tough and he had to yank at the hat. He yanked it right off my head. Before I could get it back a big piece of it was gone, and Galileo was chomping on it as though it was a delicious bunch of clover. If that is the sort of thing he eats, I can see why he looks thin. That horse is a character, and if today is any indication, life is going to be interesting around the R & G Ranch and Grover's Corner.

Saturday, June 28th

Today has certainly been a wasted day. I didn't get anything done that I had planned to do. The whole morning was spent on that crazy horse, Galileo. Something will have to be done about him or he'll have Grover's Corner in an uproar. Also he takes up too much of my time. If I am going to produce a play or a musical this summer, I can't spend my time playing baby-sitter to a horse.

I discovered that while we were away getting Galileo yesterday, Mr. Sylvester from the Princeton *Bugle* had stopped by. I had forgotten that he said he had a play written by his niece. He left it with Aunt Mabel yesterday afternoon. It was all very nicely typed and in a loose-leaf notebook. Aunt Mabel didn't remember it until this morning, and she gave it to me at breakfast.

Before I started to read the play I went to see Midge. She was limping around the barn doing things for Galileo. Her knee was wrapped in a big bandage and I guess it was stiff and sore. So was I, from riding Galileo. It wasn't as bad as the time before, though, and during the day most of the stiffness wore off. But that early in the morning I was still sore and maybe I wasn't very sympathetic about Midge's knee. She was grouchy too, but as it turned out the knee had nothing to do with it.

"I can't go to the auction sale this afternoon," she said, when I asked her what was the matter. "And tomorrow is ruined too. What's the use of owning a horse when cousins descend on you like a plague of locusts?"

"How many cousins do you have coming?" I asked. I knew a cousin was coming to spend the night but I hadn't known there was going to be a flock of them.

"One cousin," Midge said. "But when that's Eloise, it's a plague."

I didn't ask what was wrong with the cousin because I knew Midge would tell me anyway.

"Eloise is dumb, dull, overbearing, uninteresting, sloppy, ugly, fat, and silly," Midge said. "And that's not all. There's a generation gap."

All of my cousins are much older than I am and most of them are married. So I could see how there would be a generation gap. "How much older is she?" I asked.

"Three years and a half," Midge said. "But believe me, that's enough. People are always talking about the generation gap between parents and their children. They should meet Eloise. Those three and a half years seem like two hundred. She doesn't understand me and I don't understand her. As far as I'm concerned she belongs to a lost generation."

"How come she's spending the weekend with you if you don't like each other?"

"Her father, that's my mother's brother Wayne, is an electronics engineer. There's a big seminar of electronics geniuses going on in Princeton this weekend and he's attending, even if he isn't much of a genius. The whole family came along."

"And they're all staying with you?"

"No, thank heaven," Midge said. "They used to live near here and are good friends with some people named Wiggins. So my aunt and uncle and the two younger boys are staying there. They haven't got room for Eloise so I'm stuck with her. I have to help clean house this morning, I have to stay home and entertain Eloise this afternoon, and tomorrow afternoon I have to go to a party with her. I don't know most of the other girls at the party, and they're Eloise's friends, not mine. She'd rather I didn't go and I'd much rather go riding on Galileo. I'll bet Eloise's mother made her arrange it so I'd be asked, and my mother is making me go. There are times when I don't understand mothers at all!"

Midge had been planning on going to the auction sale from the moment she knew she was getting a horse. There are auction sales around Princeton, Hopewell, or Flemington every week. My Aunt Mabel loves to go to them. They often sell everything in a house when someone moves to the West Coast or someplace far away. The big attraction seems to be antiques—antique furniture, glass, dishes, or bric-a-brac. I asked Uncle Al how old something had to be to become an antique.

"That's a good question," he said, scratching his head. "I guess when it's older than whoever is bidding on it. You know, I got the wrong idea about the early settlers in America when I went to school. I thought they had a pretty rough time of it and lived in small, simple houses they built themselves. They didn't. Every last one of them must have had a great big twenty-room house."

"What do you mean?" I asked. I visited Williamsburg one time and, while there are some big houses, most of them are small with low ceilings.

"They had to have big houses to hold all the antiques that keep turning up," Uncle Al said. "Every family must have had twenty sets of dishes, too."

"He's exaggerating, Henry," Aunt Mabel said. "I suppose some of the things sold as antiques aren't old at all, and some are out-and-out fakes. But a lot of them are real, and I'm very interested in those."

Uncle Al says the auction sales are a bore but he usually goes. Aunt Mabel doesn't like to drive and Uncle Al is interested in old bottles. Now and then some are sold at auctions. The reason I wanted to go was that I'd never been to an auction. Midge was really more anxious to go than I was.

This particular sale was about four miles away.

They were selling all the contents of an old house out in the country. When they advertise a sale in the paper they list the most important items to get people to come. This one listed a lot of furniture, a slant-top desk, an antique cherry corner cupboard, a piecrust table, all sorts of Limoges china, Dresden china figures, majolica ware, and things like that. About every other word was "old" or "antique." It sounded like a pretty dull bunch of junk to me but at the end it said "harness, miscellaneous items of tack." Midge saw this and got all excited. Now that she couldn't go, she was certain she would miss some rare bargains.

"There'll probably be some beautiful bridles and halters," she complained. "Maybe even a saddle. It would be nice to have an English saddle."

"If there was a saddle, it probably would have said so," I pointed out. "I'll go, and if anything comes up that you can use and it is cheap, I'll buy it."

"I'd appreciate it," Midge said. "I've got five dollars which I can give you to take along."

"As soon as you get Galileo fed, let's sit down and talk about getting a gang together who might be interested in a play," I suggested. "I've got a play at home but before you can seriously consider a play you need to know if you can get a cast for it."

"I can't take any time this morning," Midge said. "I know you spent three or four days helping me get ready for Galileo and I really am going to help you. But Mom told me not to be gone more than ten minutes and I've already been fifteen. I have to help clean house! Aunt Carol is a real pill, she fusses about every-thing. I don't understand why people always go to so much trouble for unpleasant relatives. It ought to be the other way around—you work hard to get ready for the people you like."

I've always heard that authors, playwrights, and other creative people, such as play producers, need peaceful, relaxed surroundings so they can think well. I went home and strung up the hammock between two trees in the back yard. Then I lay back and started to read the play.

Mr. Sylvester's niece must have been a real sad, gloomy case if she was anything like her play. In about the first six lines you were told that the leading lady's husband had been killed in a terrible automobile accident. Her son was sick and seemed to be getting worse. The doctor was trying to decide if he had some horrible disease when I was interrupted by Aunt Mabel coming to the back door.

"Midge is on the telephone, Henry. She's all ex-cited about something."

I went to the telephone in the kitchen. "Galileo's gone!" Midge said.

"He's probably hiding someplace," I said. There are a few trees and bushes inside the fence.

"No, he isn't," Midge said. "The gate is open and he's gone. Would you help me look for him? I can't get around too fast with this knee."

I put the play down and started toward the barn. I stopped outside the door to call Agony, thinking he might be some help in tracking down Galileo, but he was nowhere around.

Midge was standing by the open gate to the paddock when I arrived. "Do you suppose someone was mean enough to open this and let him out?" she asked.

Mr. Glass had made the gate out of rough boards to go with the fence. It was fastened by a sliding bar. It looked complicated for a horse to figure out, but Galileo was a smart horse.

"I think he opened it," I said. "But it doesn't make much difference; we have to find him. I'll get on my bike and ride down the road a ways to see if he's headed back to where he used to live."

"I doubt if he has any idea which way to go after riding most of the way in the trailer," Midge said. "Actually I'll feel better if that's what he's done. I don't want him getting into trouble here. Did I tell you that Mr. Apple went over to see the township clerk at the Municipal Building about Galileo?"

"No. When?"

"I guess a little while after we arrived yesterday afternoon. He wanted to know if it was legal to keep a horse here. Mr. Gleason, the clerk, called Dad about it later."

"Uncle Al looked that up," I said. "There's no law against keeping any farm animal here in Grover's Corner."

"I know," Midge said. "But I don't want the Apples stirring up a fuss."

I hurried home and got out my bike. First I pedaled

up the road toward Princeton for about half a mile. I didn't see a sign of Galileo and there were no tracks on the shoulders. Of course the shoulders of the road are well covered with grass and it wouldn't be easy to see tracks. I was going past our house, headed in the other direction, when Midge came hobbling out to the road from the Millers' yard, waving her arms.

"I just heard him whinny," she said. "He's around here somewhere."

I hurried around the Millers' house and into their back yard. There, standing in the middle of Mrs. Miller's flower garden, was Galileo. Agony was lying comfortably on the grass a few feet away. They looked as happy and companionable as could be. As we got near, Galileo reached over and nipped one of Mrs. Miller's prize roses. He was very careful to avoid the thorns. He chewed on the rose a minute, and then rose petals came fluttering out of the sides of his mouth.

"Isn't he cute?" Midge said. "Maybe he thinks he has bad breath and wants to smell like a rose."

"If Mrs. Miller sees him, he'll be horse meat," I said.

I picked my way through the flowers and got hold of Galileo's halter. I led him out of the garden as carefully as I could, but he stepped on some pansies and one clump of iris.

"I don't think the Millers are home," Midge said. She looked at the clump of iris. "They'll recover."

We led Galileo back to the barn. Agony trotted

95

along beside him. He and Galileo seemed to have struck up a friendship and I could see he wasn't going to be much help tracking down the horse. He'd disappear along with him.

We put Galileo back inside the fence. I found a short piece of rope and tied it around the gate so that even if he did slide the bar back, the gate wouldn't open. Then Midge went back to cleaning house for her mother and I went back to my gloomy play with the sick boy.

I was in the middle of the second act, the son had died, and the woman's married daughter had some sort of serious trouble with her nerves, when Aunt Mabel appeared at the back door again. "Midge says he's gone again. The rope is untied!"

I really didn't mind too much when I put the play down. I was getting tired of so many sick people. This time Midge and I used strategy in finding Galileo. She called the horse and I called Agony. Agony suddenly appeared by the road in front of the Ainsworths'. We hurried in his direction and followed him around the Ainsworths' house.

Mr. Ainsworth is a retired plumber and very handy with tools. He always keeps his place in perfect order. Part of the back yard is partitioned off with a neat white picket fence. Inside the fence is his vegetable garden, which is always the best-looking vegetable garden in Grover's Corner. There's never a weed in it. He's good friends with Uncle Al and Aunt Mabel and often gives them tomatoes and beans and other vegetables. I wasn't very happy when I saw Galileo. He was standing right against the picket fence trying to reach over and eat Mr. Ainsworth's carrots. The carrots were so small that they probably didn't matter much. The trouble was that Mr. Ainsworth had just painted the picket fence and Galileo was leaning against it. I took hold of his halter and led him away a few feet.

"He's turned into a zebra!" Midge shouted and went off into gales of laughter.

Mr. Ainsworth drove in the lane in his car while we were still standing there. He walked across the yard, saw Galileo's side, and stopped with his head cocked on one side like a robin.

"What gives?" he asked.

"I'm afraid Galileo's been leaning against your freshly painted fence," Midge said. "I'm sorry."

Mr. Ainsworth walked over to look at the fence. "New type of finish for a fence, all right—half horse-hair. Well, no great harm done. I've more paint. All I need is someone to repaint it. Now just whose horse is this?"

"Mine," said Midge. "I'll be over to paint it soon but I have to stay home today."

"No hurry," said Mr. Ainsworth. "It should dry before you repaint it anyhow. If I was you I'd get some alcohol or something and try to get those stripes off that horse."

Midge took Galileo home to do some paint-removal work and I went back for the third time to my hammock and the play. People kept on having accidents and dying of horrible things so fast that I could hardly keep track. I decided long before the end that I couldn't produce that play. I would never find enough kids to take all the parts unless I resurrected some of the dead and let them play a second time. I'm going to ask Mr. Sylvester what his niece has against people that she kills them off so fast. The heroine herself was dying when Aunt Mabel appeared at the door again.

"Midge says to tell you it is a real emergency this time. She's at the barn."

I raced down to the barn. Midge was standing by the gate with a lead rope in her hand, looking worried.

"He's in the Apples' garage!" she said. "What will we do?"

"Get him out!" I said. "The quicker the better. Don't wait for the police to come."

"I don't think they know he's there yet," Midge said. "They must be varnishing the floors of the living room and dining room or something like that. They have all the furniture out on the front steps and in the yard. They're at the front of the place and Galileo went through the hedge and across the back yard."

I looked at the gate, which was still closed. "How'd he get out?" I asked.

"He was over at my house," Midge explained. "I'd just finished taking the paint off him. I used up all the rubbing alcohol in the house. He was tied up and I guess he untied the lead. How am I going to keep him in if he can open gates and untie ropes?"

"We'll figure that out later," I said. "Right now

the problem is to get him out of the Apples' garage without being seen. He's liable to walk out of his own accord any minute if we don't do something."

Midge shook her head and grinned. "There's a big drum of bird seed in the garage and he's eating that. If Mrs. Apple sees him we'll just say he's a strange variety of bird—a horse-tailed star watcher." She began giggling.

Midge has a good sense of humor but she can pick some peculiar times to go into one of her silly spells.

"What we need is some kind of diversion so they will be sure to stay at the front of their place. Then I could slip into the garage from the other side, grab Galileo, and lead him across the back to our lot here."

We decided to walk down the road past the Apples' and scout the situation. Mr. Apple was inside but Mrs. Apple was bustling back and forth, into the front yard and back into the house. Galileo was standing quietly back in the garage. I was wondering where Agony was when suddenly he appeared right beside me. He had been chased from the Apples' property several times and knew enough to stay away, even if Galileo didn't.

We were past the Apples' a short way when Midge nodded up at a big red arrow tacked to a telephone pole. "Even if my cousin weren't coming, I couldn't go to that sale. I'd have to stay home and chase Galileo."

"Does the auctioneer put those up to show people the way to the sale?" I asked.

Midge nodded. "It's straight on up this road about

four miles. Most of the people coming from Princeton will come this way." She glanced at her watch. "Eleven thirty. They ought to be coming any minute. People always go to an auction early so they can snoop around and spot all the good things."

Two cars appeared down the road and I called Agony to stay over by me. One of the cars slowed slightly and the woman driving looked at the big red arrow as she went past.

"I've got an idea," I said. "We'll change that sign and make it point right into the Apples' driveway."

Midge looked at me without changing expression for a minute and then said, "Pure genius! Henry, you're a blooming genius!"

Of course I know I have some good ideas but it's nice to have someone tell you so.

We had the sign twisted around in less than a minute and I cut across the field to a point right opposite the Apples' garage. I waited there for a chance to climb the fence and get Galileo. Midge disappeared in the shrubbery where she could watch without being seen.

We didn't have to wait long. A big van with a sign on the side saying *Alesandro's Lunch Service* came down the road, slowed as it got near the sign, hesitated, and then turned in the Apples' driveway. The Apples have a driveway that makes half a circle in front of the house and comes out the other side of the lawn. Another part goes on back to the garage. The big van pulled right up to the front door. The driver jumped out, opened the back of his van, and began taking out boxes.

Two cars were a short distance behind the van. One started to turn in the drive and then parked beside the road. The second pulled up behind the first and everyone began walking up the driveway. I could see other cars coming, and I knew that there would soon be a crowd. With that arrow and all that furniture sitting on the front lawn, unless someone knew exactly where the sale was, he was certain to be fooled. Then I heard Mrs. Apple's voice. She has one you can hear blocks away, especially when she's excited. I stopped watching and began climbing the fence.

I didn't see much of what happened. I was busy. I slipped into the garage, grabbed Galileo's halter, put the lid back on the can of bird seed, and started for home. Galileo's walk may look awkward, but it is reasonably fast, especially when you're half pulling him along. We were across the back yard in no time. I didn't waste any time hunting for the biggest gap in the hedge. I picked the first spot that I thought would do and we pushed our way through. I got two or three scratches on my arm and one on my face. I suppose Galileo did too, but he had it coming.

I put Galileo inside the pasture again, and this time I tied the gate shut with a longer piece of rope and about six knots. Then I started toward the Apples'. I met Midge about halfway.

"Show's all over!" she said. "Too bad you had to miss it. It was marvelous!"

"What happened?"

"Mrs. Apple was inside when that big lunch truck drove in. They always have a lunch table at a sale serving coffee and hot dogs and things. He figured he was at the right place and began to set up his grill and table right in the Apples' front yard. And then about ten people came wandering up the driveway. They began inspecting the furniture and making remarks about it. About this time Mrs. Apple appeared. I thought she was going to explode. Boy, did she tell everybody what she thought of them!" Midge went off into spasms of laughter. "Everyone was flabbergasted. They didn't know why she was telling them to get out. They were five minutes getting things straightened out."

"The Apples probably know about the sign, and they'll suspect us," I said.

Midge grinned happily. "I had a brilliant idea of my own," she said. "I was hiding behind that big barberry bush right by the sign. As soon as there were three or four cars parked in front of the Apples', I put the sign back the way it was. This will go down in history as the great sale mystery!"

I looked at my watch. It was time to go eat lunch if I expected to go to the sale.

"I hope this cousin of yours likes to chase after horses," I told her. "You're on your own this afternoon."

Saturday evening, June 28th

Actually it is Sunday morning as I am writing this. All I wrote last night was the date. I was too tired. I was at the auction sale all afternoon and then after dinner I went to the movies with Uncle Al and Aunt Mabel. I haven't met Midge's cousin Eloise yet. After what Midge has told me about her, I'm not in any hurry.

We had some sandwiches for lunch and left for the sale about a quarter after twelve. It was only about five minutes away so we got there in plenty of time. Both sides of the road were lined with parked cars and I thought there was a big crowd but Uncle Al said there would be many more by one.

"The advertisement said the sale would start at one thirty," he told me. "If it actually starts on time the auctioneer will sell odds and ends and junk that isn't worth much for half an hour or so. He'll wait until everyone is here."

The sale was held in the back yard of a small house. There was an acre or so of lawn and woods around the house. In back was a small barn, a garage, and another small building that I guess had been a garden house. Several tables had been placed near the back porch and they were covered with china and glass. A number of people milled around looking it over. Most of it looked old and uninteresting to me, but Aunt Mabel got quite excited about two dishes. The furniture, which was off to one side on the lawn, didn't draw much attention. There were five or six Oriental rugs, and half a dozen people were examining them. Most of the furniture was too new to be interesting, I guess.

Uncle Al was right. The auctioneer began by selling junk. There were baskets of old fruit jars, some crocks, all sorts of flowerpots, and a few worn-out garden tools. One big cardboard box was full of leather straps, pieces of bridles, several reins, and a jumble of other leather and bits. I had looked at it before the sale started and didn't know what half of it was. I did discover one halter that seemed to be in one piece. It certainly wasn't much to be advertised as "miscellaneous tack," and it came up for sale along with the junk.

"Ladies and gentlemen, we have a buggy for sale this afternoon. It is in A-1 condition and ready for use. Whoever buys it can drive it away, assuming he has had the foresight to bring a horse. Somehow we neglected to include this in our advertisement. Now, there is also a good set of harness which was advertised. In view of the fact that whoever buys the buggy will probably want the harness, we will sell both at the same time. That will be about three o'clock. In the meantime, what am I bid on this box of miscellaneous straps, brushes, and other equipment? You need it if you have a horse."

No one was much interested, and I could see why. Someone bid fifty cents and I raised the bid to seventy-five. No one else bid again. I paid for the box and began going through it. Aside from the halter, there wasn't much. At the bottom I found a big folded cloth with some straps and buckles attached. I began to unfold it, but there wasn't room. I would have covered up the woman sitting next to me.

"What do you suppose it is?" I asked Uncle Al.

"You've got me," Uncle Al said. "Wait until later when we can open it out and look at it."

"I think it's an exercise blanket," a gray-haired man several seats away volunteered. "In the wintertime they used to put big heavy blankets on a horse to keep him warm if he had to stand in the cold for a while. This is the same thing except that it is lightweight and used in the summer. After you'd ridden or driven a horse fast and he was covered with sweat, you walked him a bit to cool him off gradually, and then put an exercise blanket on him. They were also used when the flies were bothering a horse."

I refolded the exercise blanket and put it back in the box. Maybe it and the halter together were worth seventy-five cents, but there wasn't much else of any use. As I finished putting everything back, a basketful of gadgets came up for sale. The auctioneer held up an odd-looking device that he said was a potato masher. I could see several pots in the basket and what looked like the handle of a frying pan.

"Now here's a fine collection of kitchen utensils," the auctioneer said. "If there is a young bride present, all she needs to do is buy this basket and she can cook like Grandma."

The crowd laughed, but no one seemed to want the basket. I saw the edge of a metal object that I thought might be a currycomb. Besides, it is sort of fun bidding, so I said, "Twenty-five cents." The minute I did, a woman on the other side of the crowd bid fifty cents. As Uncle Al said later, you get carried away with the excitement and think you are taking something valuable away from the other bidders. Before I knew what was happening I was up to two dollars. The woman quit and there I was with a basketful of kitchen junk which cost two dollars.

One of the assistants delivered the basket and collected my money. I picked up the thing that I had thought might be a currycomb and looked at it.

"I haven't seen one like that in years," Aunt Mabel said.

"What is it?" I asked.

"A grater," she told me. "You can grate lemon peel

or things like that. My mother used to have one for grating horse-radish. We grew horse-radish in the garden and made our own horse-radish sauce. And I had to do the grating."

I was disgusted. I had spent two dollars for a horse-radish grater. I fished out a couple of knives. One had a wood handle but half of the handle was missing. The other was rusty and stained. I didn't bother going through the rest of the pots and pans and strainers to the bottom of the basket.

"I wish one of those young brides would offer me a dollar for this," I said. "I'd sell it. I don't want to cook like Grandma."

"People buy stuff at an auction they wouldn't think of buying anywhere else," Uncle Al said. "You've just proved it."

I watched other people making silly purchases for a while. At about a quarter to three the auctioneer announced that he was going to sell the furniture and then take a five-minute break to rest his voice and have a cup of coffee. They had pulled the carriage out of the barn and it was standing near a velvet sofa at the far side of the lawn. Uncle Al and I went over to look at it.

"It *is* in good condition," Uncle Al said, shaking one wheel. "I have a vague recollection of my grandfather driving around in one of these."

The buggy was black with a black top and yellow wheels. There was a jumble of straps in the back which turned out to be the harness. Mrs. Wallach had said that Galileo was broken to harness and I thought it might be fun to have a buggy. I didn't know how Midge would feel about it, however, so I decided that if I bought it, I would pay for it myself.

When the auctioneer finally offered the buggy for sale there were only three people interested. I had four and a half dollars left of Midge's money and eight dollars of my own. That didn't go very far. I made just one bid—ten dollars. The price went up in five-dollar steps to forty dollars in a few seconds. Then the two people bidding slowed down. Finally a man with a dark mustache wearing a red checked sport shirt bought it at fifty-two dollars.

I wandered around for a while, looking at the barn and the woods in back of the barn. There wasn't anything of interest, so I went back to my seat beside Aunt Mabel.

"I was looking through that basket to see what you'd bought, and down inside that old coffeepot there were twelve of these, all wrapped in paper," she said, handing me a piece of amber-colored glass.

"What is it?" I asked. The piece of glass was about an inch and a half high. The front was molded to look like a small basket of fruit and there was a narrow slot in the top.

"I think it's a place-card holder," Aunt Mabel said. "You put one in front of each place at the dinner table. The person's name is printed on a little card which goes in the slot. I've never seen any like these. I wouldn't be surprised if they were worth quite a bit."

At that moment the men began carrying things out

of the house. There were about six trunks and chests. The second one to be sold was very old, with brass handles and corners. The auctioneer opened it and pulled out some strange-looking clothes. There was a long black lace dress, a huge hat with flowers all over it, a swallow-tailed coat, a cape, a tall top hat like the one Abraham Lincoln wore, and dozens of other things. The auctioneer held up a few things for the crowd to see.

"The lucky buyer of this chest can outfit his entire family," he said. "Or have a masquerade party."

I was interested. One of the things that had been bothering me about my play was how I would get the costumes. These would have been perfect for a play taking place about the time of the Civil War.

I bid two dollars, and someone else bid three. The price went to six and I thought that everyone else had quit, when suddenly some man behind me said seven dollars. I turned around and it was the man with the mustache who had bought the buggy. Someone else joined in and I gave up. The man with the mustache finally bought the chest for thirteen dollars.

It took two of the auctioneer's helpers to carry the chest out to the buyer. By this time there were many more people than there were seats, and a number of people were standing up in back and on each side. The man with the mustache was over near one edge. I watched him as he opened the chest. He picked up several of the costumes and let them fall back with a sort of disgusted look on his face. He didn't seem very happy with what he had bought. I wondered why he had run the price up to thirteen dollars. Then I had an idea. He picked up the chest all by himself and I followed him.

He was shoving the chest out of the way under his buggy when I arrived. "Would you be interested in trading something for that?" I asked, nodding toward the chest.

"I might," he said. "I bought it because I thought my kid sister might like it. But I'm always interested in a good trade. What have you got in mind?"

"I've got twelve of these," I said, reaching in my pocket and bringing out the amber glass place-card holder.

He took it and looked at it for a minute. "Don't even know what it is," he said.

"An antique place-card holder," I said. "They're very rare."

"That could be," he agreed. "But I don't give formal dinners. And I haven't the foggiest idea whether they're worth ten dollars apiece or ten cents." He turned to look at the crowd. "I got here too late."

"What did you want?" I asked.

"Oriental rugs. Now if you had a good rug I'd be interested in a trade."

A woman sitting near Aunt Mabel had bought one of the rugs. I didn't remember what she had paid for it but I knew it was more than I had with me. However, I couldn't lose anything by trying, so I went over to where she was sitting. The rug was rolled up at her feet.

"Would you like to trade your rug for some place-card holders?" I asked.

She didn't seem a bit surprised. People at auctions are very friendly. She took the place-card holder and examined it.

"I don't know much about this, but it looks very unusual. How many do you have?"

"Twelve," I said.

"I really haven't any use for twelve place-card holders, and I'm not much of a collector," she said. "But do you see that woman over there by that tree?"

After a minute we straightened out which woman she meant. She was a middle-aged woman with a scarf tied around her hair. She was wearing slacks that she must have bought a long time ago when she was much thinner.

"That woman is an antique dealer. She'll probably appreciate these. She bought a big platter that I'd like to have. I wasn't paying attention or she would never have got it. You go make a deal with her for the platter and then I'll trade you for the rug."

By this time I figured out that most people at auctions buy things that they wish they could trade for something else. And of course I was one of them. I went over to the antique dealer, told her who I was, and showed her my place-card holder.

"I have twelve," I said.

"Good for you," she said. She looked at it very carefully. "What do you want for them?"

"I'll trade all twelve for that platter," I said.

She had several boxes of china on the ground beside her. There was only one platter. It was a huge white one with an orange design on it. It would have looked good holding a roast turkey.

"If they are all in good condition, it's a trade," she agreed.

I went back for my coffeepot. I took them out and unwrapped them. One had a tiny little chip in it. She looked at it for a minute but finally decided that the chip didn't matter.

"It's your platter," she said, handing it to me.

"Do you mind telling me what you paid for this?" I asked.

"Forty-two dollars," she said promptly.

I almost dropped my forty-two-dollar platter when I heard that. I walked over to the woman with the Oriental rug, carrying the platter very carefully. I handed it to her for inspection. "I've got the platter; can I examine the rug?"

We moved away from the crowd and she unrolled the rug. I don't know anything about Oriental rugs, but this one looked nice, and it didn't have any holes in it. This time I thought I'd ask about the price first.

"What did you have to pay for it?" I asked.

"Fifty-five dollars."

It wasn't a very big rug. I wouldn't ever have paid fifty-five dollars for it. Of course I don't have any use for a rug, but then I don't have any use for a platter either.

"Could you give me two dollars extra?" I asked.

"That's an odd amount," she said after a minute, "but I do want that platter. I guess so."

I put the two dollars in my pocket and the rug on my shoulder and went over to the buggy. With the two dollars back that I had paid for the basket of junk, I figured I couldn't lose. At the rate I was going I might even get rich.

"Well, I managed to trade my place-card holders for an Oriental rug," I told the man with the mustache.

He unrolled it, looked at both sides, and then said, "Well, want to trade?"

He'd only paid thirteen dollars for the chest and my rug was worth fifty-five dollars. "My rug is worth a good deal more," I said. "I need something to boot."

"I'm not so sure about that," he said. "If you tried to buy a new buggy like this you'd probably have to pay three hundred dollars. That harness is worth a good seventy-five. And it's not as hard to find buyers as you think. There are more people around with horses every day."

I looked at him with my mouth open. When I had nodded at the chest he had thought I meant the buggy. I couldn't decide for a minute whether to tell him the truth or keep my mouth shut and take the buggy. Since I had my two dollars back I would be getting the buggy and harness for nothing.

"Tell you what," he said. "I bought that old pine chest and it's full of clothes. There's an old quilt in there that might have some value. I want the chest, but I'll throw in the stuff that's in it."

We agreed. I found two empty cardboard boxes and we took all the clothes out of the chest and put them in the boxes. I put the two boxes in the back of the buggy and went back to join Uncle Al and Aunt Mabel.

"Where have you been?" Uncle Al asked. "Some rare old rusty dueling swords were just sold for six dollars."

I explained what I had been doing and that I now had the buggy, the harness, the costumes, and my two dollars back. Uncle Al rummaged around in my basket and came up with the knife with half a handle.

"Here," he said. "You might as well go trade for the swords."

Sunday, June 29th

We didn't bring the buggy home until today. The sale wasn't over until after five. Aunt Mabel was interested in an old china clock and it wasn't sold until almost the end. Then she didn't get it because it went too high. After she had spent all afternoon there, you would have thought that she would have been disappointed, but she didn't seem to mind.

Uncle Al considered tying the buggy on behind the car, but he didn't have any strong rope.

"If it should get loose, it might get wrecked," he said. "The sensible thing to do is come back tomorrow with the horse and drive it home. I'll come with you and help you hitch up Galileo and see that he behaves. I want to see the auctioneer now and make certain that it's all right to leave the buggy in the barn overnight."

We went to the movies after dinner, but before we left I walked over to tell Midge about the buggy. No one was home. At breakfast this morning Aunt Mabel suggested that I surprise Midge with it. That seemed like a good idea, but I needed some excuse for borrowing Galileo. She would notice he was gone and think he had escaped again. I went over to her house about nine thirty this morning but she was gone again.

"Her aunt and uncle came by and took her and Eloise to church," Mrs. Glass said. "They are all going out for dinner at noon, and then Eloise and Margaret are going to a party at the Gilpins'."

"What time will she be home?" I asked.

"I'm supposed to pick her up at four thirty," Mrs. Glass said. "The Gilpins are only a mile or so up the road, so we should be home by a quarter to five. Why? Is there something important?"

"I wondered if it would be all right if I borrowed Galileo this afternoon," I said.

"Why, of course! She considers Galileo as much your horse as hers. After all, you are supplying the place to keep him."

I saddled up Galileo about three o'clock. He seemed bored with being in the pasture and glad to go somewhere. We trotted down the road at a good clip without my having to urge him. About a mile before I got to the place where the sale had been, I passed a mailbox with the name "Gilpin" on it. There were some fancy brick posts at the end of the driveway but the house was hidden in the trees. I figured Midge was probably there at her party, but she couldn't see me and I couldn't see her.

Uncle Al was waiting for me when I arrived. Mr. Ainsworth was with him.

"I remembered that George's father used to have a blacksmith shop," Uncle Al said. "I figured he would know how to hitch up a horse if anyone would."

It was a good thing Mr. Ainsworth was along. Uncle Al and I might have figured out how to put on the harness eventually, but it wouldn't have been easy. Mr. Ainsworth even knew the names of the various parts like the traces, the hames, and the terrets. It took us about fifteen minutes to get the harness on Galileo and to hitch him to the buggy. He stood quietly and seemed to know what he was doing as well as Mr. Ainsworth did.

Mr. Ainsworth got in the buggy and drove up the road a short distance. "He behaves very nicely," he said as he stopped in the yard again. "I'd drive home with you but we've got some people coming to see us and I have to get back. One of these days I'd like to borrow the rig and take my wife for a drive. Wouldn't be surprised if you could work up a nice business renting this out to people who have almost forgotten what a buggy ride is like."

Uncle Al and Mr. Ainsworth waited until I had driven a short distance, and then they went on home. I had driven almost a mile when I remembered Midge's box full of tack. I had left it in the barn. I drove back and loaded it in the back of the buggy with my two boxes of costumes. By the time I got near the Gilpins' it was after four. Midge was probably drinking a cold drink and eating ice cream, and I was driving along the road, hot and thirsty, taking her box full of tack home for her. I decided that it would serve her right if I really surprised her with the buggy. I stopped and rummaged through the boxes of old clothes until I found the tall top hat. I put it on. It was too big and came down until the brim rested on my ears, but I could still see by tilting my head back. I said "Giddap" to Galileo, and we went trotting into the Gilpins' fancy lane.

The drive wound through the trees and ended up in a circle in front of a very swank house with tall white pillars. I felt as if I was driving up to a Southern mansion. No one was in sight, and I was about to get down to ring the doorbell when a boy of about twelve came around the corner of the house. He stopped short and looked at the buggy, at Galileo, and then at me.

"Are you for real?" he asked finally.

I lifted my hat a little so I could see him better. "I'm the Mad Hatter," I said. "How about doing me a favor?"

"Like what?"

"Go tell a girl named Margaret Glass that I have come to drive her home."

"They're in the middle of ice cream and cake," he said. "Give me a little ride and then I'll go tell her."

He climbed in and we drove around the circle and

back out to the road. We went to the nearest corner, turned around and drove back. On the way we worked out a good routine. He didn't know Midge so we decided he should just go back to the patio and announce, "Miss Glass's carriage is waiting."

He must have made quite a production of it. A minute later about fifteen girls came around the house. They all started laughing and screaming when they saw Galileo, the buggy, and me sitting there with my top hat. I looked around with my nose high in the air so I could see. I kept my face perfectly straight.

It was a good thing that Midge's stuffy cousin was along, or I wouldn't have embarrassed anyone with my surprise. I should have known nothing would bother Midge. She looked at the buggy and at me and started grinning.

"Wow!" she said. "Terrific, Henry! That's cool! Can I drive?"

She climbed up in the buggy but Eloise didn't seem very anxious to follow her. In fact, she looked at Galileo and me as though she smelled something terrible.

"Come on, Eloise," Midge said. "Galileo is champing at the bit."

Eloise is several years older than Midge. It's funny how some girls suddenly seem to get dignified and stodgy when they get to be about sixteen or seventeen. Maybe she was always that way. The buggy is sort of high above the ground. To get in you step on a little iron step that hangs down from the side of

119

the buggy. Midge had got in without a second glance, but Eloise seemed to be scared of taking that first step. Finally, with two girls helping her, she managed to get in. She sat down gingerly as though she expected the buggy to fall apart any minute. It was a tight fit with three of us in that narrow buggy seat, but she had no right to complain. She took up at least her share of space.

Midge stood up, bowed in all directions, and said, "Farewell, my friends. I had a wonderful time but, alas, I must leave. Westward ho, Galileo!"

We were heading east and Galileo wasn't champing at the bit. He was champing on something else, though. He had reached out and taken off a branch of a small bush that was growing beside the driveway. He chewed on it several times and then went *Pbpbpbpbpbpbpb!* Galileo has big sloppy lips, and when he blows his breath out between them like that, things splatter all over. Two girls in white dresses jumped back and just missed being covered with wet pieces of leaves.

"All right then, if you won't westward ho, giddap!" Midge said, slapping Galileo's back with the reins.

Galileo went trotting down the lane. As soon as we were well out of sight, I took off my top hat. It was hot and uncomfortable, down almost over my eyes that way.

"Cool, Henry!" Midge said. "Driving a buggy is super!"

Monday, June 30th

I didn't make much progress today with my plans to produce a play, but the R & G Ranch made ten dollars with Galileo and the buggy. I wouldn't be surprised if we get a lot more customers, because I think Galileo will soon be famous.

After I drove Midge and her cousin home yesterday afternoon, I started to unhitch Galileo. Midge rushed home, changed into blue jeans, and came over to help me. I showed her how the harness came off. I wasn't a very good teacher, because I couldn't remember exactly how Mr. Ainsworth had put it on. We were puzzling things out together when a car stopped in front of the barn and a girl came over.

"She's one of the girls from this afternoon," Midge said to me. "I think her name is Shirley. I didn't know many of them; they were Eloise's friends."

"Hi!" the girl said. "I thought coming for Midge with a horse and buggy was a wonderful idea. Who does it belong to?"

"It's sort of a joint affair," I said. "Galileo belongs to Midge and I bought the buggy yesterday afternoon."

"Would you like to make some money with them?" she asked.

"Sure," Midge said. "Horses have to eat."

"Well, my brother is helping organize a protest march tomorrow in Princeton. I thought it would be a great idea to use the buggy in the parade. I called Jim and he said to stop by and find out if you would be interested. This is a volunteer project on the part of the Princeton students, but they have a little money. They can give you ten dollars."

"For how long?" Midge asked.

"I don't suppose it will last more than half an hour or maybe forty-five minutes. They are going to start on the campus by the library and march up Nassau Street to Morven."

"What's Morven?" I asked.

"That's the governor's mansion," Midge explained. "The capitol building is in Trenton but the governor's mansion is in Princeton. It's not far from the Princeton campus."

"What's this march protesting against?" I asked. Every time I listen to the news on the radio or read the paper, somebody is protesting against something. For all I knew the students of Princeton might be asking the governor to outlaw ice cream.

"That's right," Midge said. "Henry and Galileo and I have high principles. We're particular about what we protest against."

"You're safe," Shirley said. "This protest is against pollution. The students are going to march to Morven, as I said. They know the governor will be home at lunchtime. When he comes to the door, they are going to read a resolution asking for tougher laws against water pollution, and for a law requiring all cars to have some sort of device to keep gasoline fumes from polluting the air. I don't know whether you know it or not, but New Jersey is the most thickly populated state in the nation."

"Too many people and not enough horses," Midge said.

We agreed to take part in the march provided we didn't get overruled at home. Midge's father was doubtful at first. He said we didn't know how Galileo would act in a crowd, but finally he agreed after he had talked to Uncle Al.

"Cars don't seem to bother that horse at all," Uncle Al said. "A big truck went roaring down the road while George Ainsworth was driving him and he paid no attention at all. I'm sure he'll be safe."

"I think I'll go watch the march," Aunt Mabel said. "I may even join it."

Aunt Mabel's pet peeve is people who throw paper cups, bottles, cans, and that kind of junk out of car windows. She always tries to get their license numbers. When she does, she reports them.

Jim Albert, Shirley's brother, called after dinner

last night to make certain that we were going to the parade. I agreed to meet him at the circle in front of the Firestone Library at eleven. He said that would give them plenty of time to fasten a sign to the buggy.

This morning Midge and I hitched up Galileo without too much trouble. However, we drove over to Mr. Ainsworth's and had him check everything to see that we had done it right. Then we drove into Princeton. Galileo behaved perfectly. The traffic didn't bother him, and neither did all the students milling around in front of the Firestone Library. He bothered some of the students, though. Galileo likes hats. I thought when he took that bite out of my hat that it was because it was made of straw. But he seems to like *any* kind of hat. Most of the students were bareheaded, but those with hats didn't get close to Galileo twice.

The sign was a work of art. Three students fastened a pole at the front of the buggy and another at the back. These were wired in place so they couldn't fall down and then the sign, on a big strip of canvas, was strung between them. Both ends of the sign showed clouds of black fumes floating upward. Between the clouds it said, *"Must We Return to the Horse and Buggy to Eliminate Gasoline Fumes?"*

I had brought my camera and I took pictures of Midge holding the reins as though she were driving. Then she took several of me. As it turned out, we needn't have bothered, because there were pictures of both of us in the papers.

The march started promptly at twelve. About fifteen students had formed a band and they went first. I doubt if they had played together much, but they were loud, and the two drummers were good. Then came about a hundred students marching four abreast. They were followed by several pairs of students carrying signs on tall poles. These read, *"Stop Stream Pollution,"* *"Control Industrial Wastes,"* and things like that. Then came our buggy. Right behind us was the leader of the protest, riding in a convertible with the top down. Following him were at least a hundred more marchers. It was a bang-up parade and everyone along Nassau Street turned out to watch. Policemen were at the traffic lights and turned them green to let the parade go by. Galileo had a wonderful time. He pranced along with his head in the air and tried to keep time to the music. I think the only one who had a better time than Galileo was Midge. She waved to friends all along the way like a politician campaigning. You would have thought the whole affair was in her honor.

By the time we got to the fork where Nassau Street becomes Stockton, we had almost as big a crowd of spectators as we had students. I don't know whether the governor knew we were coming or not, but everyone else did. Morven was alive with people. There were newsmen, cameramen, and state police everywhere.

The car carrying the spokesman for the protest stopped directly in front of the main entrance. Since we were just ahead of his car, we could see and hear everything.

The leader of the protest was a tall blond student with a little scraggly goatee. It made him look as if his chin was dirty but he spoke very well. "We would like to speak to the governor," he told one of the state troopers who was standing near the entrance. "Ask him if he would be so kind as to step outside. Unless, of course, he would prefer that we all come in."

"I doubt that," the officer said. He nodded to a man standing just outside the door.

Unless the governor was deaf, he knew we were there. He was probably waiting for us, because he appeared almost immediately. He looked around, waved, and smiled, and then when the shouting had died down he asked, "What can I do for you young people?"

"Your Honor, I would like to read a resolution signed by more than four hundred Princeton students," the tall blond boy said. The governor nodded, and the spokesman produced several sheets of paper and began reading.

"Whereas man has increasingly despoiled his environment, polluted his streams, poisoned his soil, destroyed the natural beauty of the countryside and the balance of nature; and, Whereas New Jersey is one of the most thickly populated areas in the world; and, Whereas. . . ." I can't remember all of it but it went on at some length about pollution, especially from the exhausts of cars. The resolution was very well written and everyone was quiet while it was being read. That is, everyone except Galileo.

There were photographers everywhere, taking pictures of the governor, of the speaker, of the signs, and especially of Galileo and the buggy. One newspaperman with a notebook stood right in front of Galileo. He was chomping on a long black cigar. I thought the cigar was out, because he seemed to be chewing on it rather than smoking it. I guess Galileo thought so too. By this time I had begun to recognize the funny way Galileo cocked his head when he was about to do something. I saw what was coming and nudged Midge. Galileo took the cigar from the reporter's mouth so fast that he didn't know what had happened. He looked blankly first one way, then another, with his mouth open in surprise. Then he saw the end of the cigar sticking out of one side of Galileo's mouth.

"Hey, what's the idea of stealing my cigar?" he asked in a loud voice.

The speaker paused to get his breath just at that moment, so everyone within fifty feet heard and turned to see what had happened.

Of course, Galileo didn't answer. He kept right on chewing on the cigar and the last of it disappeared. I think the end of it must have been smoldering, or maybe tobacco is too strong even for Galileo. He began coughing in huge rasping coughs. I'm positive that smoke came out with that first cough, and Midge says it did too. But regardless of what came out with the first cough, chewed pieces of tobacco came out with the second and third coughs. Horses have a lot of saliva in their mouths, and Galileo's mouth had probably been watering anyhow as he eyed that cigar. The pieces of tobacco were about half the size of my little fingernail, and they were wet. What Galileo did to that poor reporter shouldn't happen to anyone. His face looked as though he had the black measles, and his white shirt turned polka-dot. He was wearing glasses, so none of the tobacco got in his eyes, which was lucky. I don't suppose he could see very well, though, until he had wiped off his glasses. He didn't say a word for a minute and then he groaned. "I don't believe it!" he said finally.

The speaker looked at the reporter and then at Galileo. He paused only a few seconds and then he said, "And, Whereas the air is so foul even here in our beautiful city of Princeton that a noble animal like the horse can't breathe properly and is in danger of coughing his head off, we submit that remedial legislation must be passed at the next session of the Legislature."

"That was a very persuasive resolution and a convincing demonstration," the governor said with a smile.

I think more pictures were taken of Galileo than of the governor. He stole the show. They took stills and movie shots of him and then some of the buggy and the sign. The speaker had a few more words to say about the legislation the students felt was necessary. Then the governor made a short speech. He agreed that pollution was a very serious problem and he mentioned what he had done and hoped to do about it. In the middle of his speech Midge waved at someone. I

128

looked over and there was Officer Haywood. When the governor finished his speech, which was much shorter than the resolution, Haywood walked over to the buggy.

"You turn up at some of the oddest times and places," he said. "How come you're here? You're not a Princeton student."

"We're outside consultants," Midge said. "Specialists."

"Trouble specialists, I'm beginning to believe," Haywood said. "Stay out of mischief or I'll give you a ticket."

"I like that! Trouble specialists!" Midge said to me. "And after all the help I gave him when he was investigating that mysterious body. Telling me to stay out of mischief as if I was five years old!"

All the state police guarding Morven were wearing broad-brimmed hats like those of the National Park Service. I guess they are made of felt and they must taste awful, but I could tell that Galileo was interested.

"If he gets any closer, Galileo will get even for you," I said.

Galileo stretched out his neck but Officer Haywood was too far away. I forgot about the hat, but Galileo didn't. The student in charge of the parade signaled for us to start moving. Midge slapped Galileo with the reins. He took one step forward, veered two steps to the right, and stretched his long neck. His teeth clamped down on Officer Haywood's hat brim and he tossed his head. He took off that hat as neat as can be.

He didn't miss a single step, but kept walking briskly down the drive with the hat in his teeth.

"Come back with my hat!" Haywood shouted.

He ran after Galileo and a cameraman ran after both of them, taking pictures as he went. The hat must have been tough, or maybe Galileo decided it didn't have a good flavor. When Haywood caught up and grabbed the hat, Galileo let him take it. The brim was a mess—all wet and crumpled—but the hat was still in one piece.

We marched back up Nassau Street and disbanded by the library. Two newspapermen were there and Midge and Galileo and I had our pictures taken a few more times. We collected our ten dollars and started home.

"Tomorrow we've got to get started on our plans for that play," I said to Midge. "We aren't making any progress at all."

"Do you suppose we could find a play that would have a part for a horse?" she asked. "Galileo likes to act."

Midge gets some silly ideas.

Monday, July 7th

I have just come back from Baltimore, where I visited my father's older sister for almost a week. Her husband is dead and her two children are grown, so she lives by herself. She is very nice and did everything she could to see that I had a good time. Still, with no one my age around, I felt sort of lonesome. I am glad to be back in Grover's Corner.

My Aunt Helen teaches English literature in the Baltimore school system, and she was very interested in my idea of putting on a play. She has coached a number of plays at her school and was able to give me a lot of good advice.

"The idea of a summer theater group is excellent," she said. "But be certain that you get a group together that is interested enough to practice regularly. In the summer, people have a habit of going off suddenly to the seashore or the mountains or somewhere. And I can tell you that most young people, if they have to choose between your play and going surfing, will pick the surf every time. Even during the school year I always have trouble keeping my cast together. I think I am all set and then the roof caves in."

"What sort of things happen?" I asked.

"Well, one year the girl who was to play the lead—and she was excellent—suddenly had to have braces on her teeth. She flatly refused to appear on stage with braces. And the boy who was to play the star male role broke his ankle skiing."

Aunt Helen gave me a play to read that one of the boys in her high-school English class had written. It was about three boys and a girl who formed a musical group. Their parents didn't take them seriously and thought their orchestra was just a hobby. They had all sorts of problems and got into a number of funny situations. Finally at the end they were so popular that they appeared on TV and made a number of records. It was a very good play and one that wouldn't be too difficult to produce, so Aunt Helen called the author. He said we could produce it without charge. All he wanted was to know how people liked it.

The day before I left Baltimore, Aunt Helen took me over to the Smithsonian Institution in Washington, D.C. The Smithsonian is really a group of museums with all sorts of branches. You could spend weeks there if you looked at everything. I was there once

134

before but I didn't get to the natural history museum. We had planned to see the animal exhibits first on this trip, but we got sidetracked in the paleontology and geology sections. The prehistoric animals, fossils, and rocks were so interesting that we spent the whole day there. When we left, Aunt Helen bought me a paperback book about fossils and one on geology. I'm going to hunt for fossils around Grover's Corner after I've produced my play and have more time. Uncle Al sent me a newspaper story several years ago about some boy in junior high school finding real dinosaur tracks near Princeton, so there must be fossils too.

We also went to several museums in Baltimore. My Aunt Helen likes museums. I do too, but not quite that much. By the end of the week I was glad to get back to Grover's Corner. All in all, it was not an exciting week, but it was fun and, best of all, I got a play which I can produce.

Midge said nothing had happened in Grover's Corner except that Galileo had got out twice. That horse is a regular escape artist. The first time he got out we tied a rope around the gate and the gate post. He untied that and slid back the bar. Next we tied about six knots in the rope. He wasn't able to untie it, but he chewed the rope in two. After that Mr. Glass got a special hook at the hardware store and put it on the gate. Galileo wasn't able to get that open and for a few days he stayed where he belonged. But it seems he found a new way to get out while I was in Baltimore. Midge says she is certain the gate was locked both times. She thinks he jumped the fence. If that is the case, I don't know how she will be able to keep him in.

Midge complains about Galileo's getting out, but she is proud of how smart he is. I agree that Galileo is smart, he seems to have a sense of humor, and he's a crazy character for a horse. I like him, but he is still an ungainly, peculiar-looking critter. Midge thought so too when I went away to Baltimore, but in the week I was away there has been a big change. Now she's so sold on Galileo, she thinks he's handsome. When she shows someone her horse now, she gets upset if they hint that he might not win a beauty contest. Midge has a good sense of humor, but she has lost it as far as Galileo is concerned. I suppose that is what happens when you are crazy about horses and get one of your own.

Tuesday, July 8th

The R & G Ranch has a real problem on its hands. Actually it is Midge's problem, since Galileo is her horse, but since we're partners I feel responsible too.

Last night, just as I was about to go to bed, there was a horrible screech from the road in front of our house—the kind tires make when someone slams on the brakes and slides about fifty feet. I didn't hear any crash so I figured that whoever had stopped so suddenly had done it in time. However, I ran out in front to see what had happened. There, standing by the side of the road, was Galileo. A few feet away was a car with its engine running and its lights on. I walked up to Galileo and took hold of his halter.

"Do you know whose horse that is?" a voice asked from the car.

"He belongs to someone up the road," I said. "I'll see that he gets back."

"You'd better tell whoever owns him to keep him off the road," the man said in an annoyed voice. "He'll get killed, or some driver will, trying to avoid him."

The car drove off and I started toward the barn with Galileo. I saw a flashlight and a minute later Midge appeared. She was wearing pajamas and a bathrobe.

"Is he all right?" she asked.

"He's all right, but that car almost hit him," I told her. "And the driver didn't like it."

"I heard those tires screech and I had a sinking feeling that Galileo might be out on the road," Midge said. "Whoever was driving that car shouldn't have been going so fast."

"Horses shouldn't be walking around on the roads at night either," I told her. "You can't blame the driver."

"This is a thickly settled area and people should drive slowly," Midge said, convinced that her horse couldn't be wrong. "There ought to be a big sign at each end of Grover's Corner."

"Look, the only sign that would do any good is a flashing sign that says, 'Look Out! A Crazy Horse Might Be Wandering Around in the Dark.' I doubt if the highway department is going to put that up."

"Well, I've tried everything I know to keep him in," Midge said. "I hate to tie him in his stall all night. It's so hot inside."

When we got to the ranch we found the gate locked

and no sign of how he got out. The only safe thing to do was to tie him in the barn. Midge had just bought a new lead rope, and we decided he couldn't chew through that in one night. And it was long enough that I was able to fasten it to a ring behind the manger where he couldn't reach the knot.

This morning after breakfast I went down to the ranch to look around. I made a complete circuit of the fence, looking at the ground very carefully. I thought that if he had jumped the fence he might have left some hoofprints on the other side where he landed. But it hasn't rained for several days and the ground is hard. I couldn't find anything. There is one section of fence at the back corner near the Apples' that is lower than the other sections. The two posts were set too deep in the ground and the top rail was very warped. This made the center of the rail about six inches lower than anywhere else. Midge came over and we dug up the two posts, turned the rail the other way so the curve would be up instead of down, and put the posts back in again, only not so deep.

"Do you think this is where he got out?" Midge asked anxiously.

"I don't know," I admitted. "But it could be."

"I wish I could make certain that if he did get out again, people would see him at night," Midge said.

"The only way to do that would be to get some lights and strap them on him," I suggested. "A headlight and a taillight."

"There are dumber ideas," Midge said after a minute. "I'm going to put that exercise blanket on him. You know, the one you bought at the sale. At least it's white. The bugs won't bother him so much, either."

We got out the exercise blanket and tried it on Galileo. It fit as well as anything is apt to fit that horse, but one of the straps that buckled across his chest had come unsewn. Midge went home for some heavy thread and a big needle to fix that. When she came back she was carrying a small can of paint and a paint brush.

"I had a brilliant idea," she said. "I was thinking about his having a headlight and a taillight, and I remembered that Dad has some luminous paint. He was always tripping over that one step back by the garage so he painted it with luminous paint. It worked very well. That was two years ago and the step still glows at night."

I took the can from her and read the label. "It says here that you should avoid getting any on your hands or skin. If you do, you should wash it off immediately with turpentine, soap, and water. You can't put this on Galileo."

"I wasn't thinking of putting it on him," Midge said. "But we could paint a big sign on the side of his exercise blanket."

While she sewed the strap, I went home for a charcoal pencil. It's always better to sketch out a sign before you paint it because it's much easier to get the letters spaced right.

Mr. Sylvester of the Princeton *Bugle* stopped by while I was in the house and I returned his niece's play. I thanked him but explained that it was too sad—that what I had been looking for was a comedy.

"To tell the truth, I thought it was sad in more ways than one," Mr. Sylvester said. "In fact, I would call it a disaster. I thought maybe I didn't appreciate it because of this generation gap I have heard so much about. I'm happy to know that someone nearer her age thinks it's awful too."

When I got back to the barn, Midge had gone. There was a note pinned to the blanket. "Had to go to Princeton for a dental appointment. Ugh! Will you please put a sign on each side? Thanks. Midge."

I looked at the blanket and decided it wouldn't be much fun to paint something ordinary like "Stop" on it. So I went home again and got my book on fossils. It is filled with pictures of prehistoric animals or what someone thought prehistoric animals looked like. I thumbed through it and picked out a Tyrannosaurus. According to my book this was one of the largest dinosaurs and sometimes was fifty feet long. I painted a baby Tyrannosaurus on one side of Galileo's blanket. I couldn't tell whether I had done a good job or not, because the paint practically disappeared on the cloth. A mother Tyrannosaurus might not have recognized it as her baby, but then she might not have recognized herself in my book either.

The dinosaur was on the left side of the blanket. For the right side I decided on a saber-toothed tiger.

I drew just the head—an enormous tiger face with huge tusks. The mouth was wide open ready to take a big bite of something. I hung the blanket to dry in the sun, saddled Galileo, and went for a ride.

The day that I fell off Ginger and had a nosebleed, I had noticed a cliff on the far side of the stream. I hadn't paid too much attention to it that day because my mind was on other things. According to my fossil book a good place to look for fossils is where a cliff has been formed by a stream and several layers of rock are exposed. I decided to investigate.

I located the cliff without any trouble. After cutting away the hill to form the cliff, the stream must have shifted its course farther away. Books on geology and fossils talk about things happening as though it took only a short time. Then when you read farther you find that it took fifty thousand years. Maybe in fifty thousand years the stream had moved away from the cliff three or four hundred yards. Anyhow, I forded the stream and started toward the ledge of rock. What had looked like a nice green pasture from the other side turned out to be a swampy bog. The grass was all marsh grass. Even with his big feet, Galileo sank in eight or ten inches. It didn't seem to bother him. The only trouble was that each time he pulled a foot out of the goo he gave it a sort of flip and a shower of mud went five feet into the air. I'm glad that I wasn't on a horse behind him. As it was, I got fairly well splattered and Galileo was a mess. His stomach was almost solid mud.

The cliff looked very promising but I didn't spend too much time actually looking for fossils. I decided I'd better get back and clean up Galileo. Most of the mud was dry by the time I got to the ranch and the clean-up job wasn't as bad as I expected. The blanket that I had painted was dry. I shook it out well and most of the charcoal marks disappeared. I decided to say nothing about what I had painted on it but let Midge be surprised.

I went down to the barn, I mean the ranch, after dinner. Midge was there putting the blanket on Galileo. He looked silly in a blanket on a hot summer night even if the blanket is only a thin cloth. He seemed to like it, though, and went trotting around the pasture with his nose in the air.

"That paint certainly doesn't show up much," Midge said. "But then it never does until it gets dark."

She said she planned to check on Galileo just before she went to bed. I thought I would too, to see how my dinosaur and tiger looked and to find out if she was surprised, but I got interested in a TV program and forgot. The next thing I knew, Midge was at the door.

"He's gone again," she said, very worried. "I hope that luminous paint does some good. If a car hits Galileo I'll just die."

I got a flashlight and went to help her hunt for him. The Glasses had guests but Mr. Glass came out to help anyhow. He and Midge took one side of the road and I took the other. We decided the first thing to do was make certain he wasn't on the road before we started hunting in neighbors' back yards. I got on my bike and rode up past the Apples' house. On my way back I saw a luminous dinosaur in the Apples' garage. It stood out very clearly because the garage was dark inside. In fact it looked so spooky that it gave me the shivers.

The Apples must have been out, because their house was also dark. I put my fingers to my mouth and gave three shrill whistles, the signal we had agreed upon. Midge was not too far away and she answered immediately. I put my bike in the ditch where it would be safe and walked down the driveway to get Galileo. He didn't try to run away and I took his halter and led him toward the road. Midge met me at the entrance to the drive.

"Wow!" she said when she saw Galileo from the side. "If that doesn't scare a driver to death it sure ought to make him stop!"

We took Galileo to the barn and decided the only safe thing to do was tie him in his stall again. We took the blanket off because it was hot inside. Midge was holding the flashlight and I was folding the blanket when there was a voice from the door.

"I might have known," the voice said. "I should have looked for you two the minute I got here."

It was Officer Haywood of the state police. He was carrying an electric lantern. He walked over and focused the beam on Galileo.

"Has he been running around loose?" he asked.

"We just caught him," I said.

"Good thing you did," Haywood said. "He would get killed out on the road. As it is, he scared some woman half out of her wits. I suppose it must have been him. I can't think of any other logical explanation."

"Who was that?" Midge asked.

"A Mrs. Beauchamp up the street," Haywood said. "She called and said a horrible monster went right by her window."

"Then it's ridiculous to think it was Galileo," Midge said. "Does he look like a monster?"

"After what he did to my hat, yes," Haywood said. He looked at Galileo very carefully. "Of course it would be easier to think this horse was a monster in the daytime than at night."

Midge didn't think he was funny. "Just what did she say this monster looked like?" she asked in a very huffy voice.

"It's amazing how the imagination can distort things, especially on a dark night when one gets a scare. Mrs. Beauchamp told me in considerable detail about a monster with a huge open mouth and big curving tusks or teeth."

"Would you like to examine Galileo's teeth?" Midge asked, still mad.

"No, thank you," Haywood said with a grin. "I've done enough looking for one night. All I ask is that you keep that horse locked up."

Wednesday, July 9th

Officer Haywood was back again today. He's a good egg and he's very smart too. Midge and I were down at the corral trying to figure out how Galileo got out. We had given up and were talking about whom to invite to our party when Haywood appeared.

"Figured out how your horse got out?" he asked Midge.

"No, we didn't," Midge said in disgust. "He's a magician or he has wings. Did you find your monster?"

"No. I'm satisfied it was the horse. I went back to Mrs. Beauchamp's this morning. She waters her flower garden every day and the ground is quite soft. I found tracks—plain ordinary prints made by a horseshoe. But she insists she saw this enormous fiery tiger. And this morning she told me that several minutes later she saw something that looked like a dinosaur." Haywood shook his head. "She's quite elderly. She's not a little off her rocker, is she?"

Midge looked at me, hesitated, and then decided it was best to tell the truth. "No. There's nothing wrong with Mrs. Beauchamp. Her eyes aren't too good and she has to wear big thick glasses. But her mind is all right."

"I think we'd better tell him," I said. I felt pretty proud that Mrs. Beauchamp had recognized both my tiger and my dinosaur.

"If we turn state's witness do we get off free?" Midge asked.

"What are you two talking about?" Haywood asked.

We explained about the blanket. He was sort of annoyed, but he thought it was funny too. "I suppose I'd better go back and tell her that we were both right. It was a horse but it was a couple of fiery monsters too. From now on you've *got* to keep that horse in. Let's look around and see if we can discover where he got out."

He went around the entire fence with us and inspected the gate. Then he scratched his head a minute, looked at the ground outside the front door of the barn, and went back inside. We followed and watched while he inspected the latch to Galileo's stall and the one on the barn's front door.

"He *is* a smart horse," Haywood said. "I think he comes in through the open door from the pasture to

147

his stall, then opens the door to his stall, which lets him into the front part of the barn. Then he opens the front door to the barn and he's out. The door to his stall swings shut by itself. Maybe the wind blew the front door shut. In any event, when they are both shut again, there is nothing to show how he got out."

"He's smart enough to shut the doors behind himself just to fool us," Midge said.

After Officer Haywood left, Midge and I put an extra hook on Galileo's stall door and another on the outside of the front door. He can't open either. I hope the mystery is finally solved.

Thursday, July 10th

Galileo hasn't got out again and no one has reported any more monsters around Grover's Corner. Midge hasn't had to go check up on him every ten minutes, so she has had time to read the play that I brought back from Baltimore. She thinks it's great too. For the first time she is showing some real interest in my idea of putting on a show.

There are eleven characters in the play. One of them must know how to play a guitar, one the drums, and one a horn. We can change the horn to some other instrument without too much trouble if we have to. The heroine has to be able to sing.

"It's not going to be easy," Midge warned. "You may think so, but I've talked to a number of my friends already. Some are going away later. Vacations rule out a lot of our best possibilities. And some aren't much interested in doing a lot of work on a play in the middle of the summer. Many of the older boys have summer jobs and so do some girls. Most kids would rather be outdoors."

"This is going to be outdoors," I pointed out.

"I know, but memorizing a part for a play is too much like schoolwork for some. However, we'll try. I think I know a boy who can take the hardest part, the part of Slim with his guitar. And there are some others that I know from the school orchestra who can play other instruments. They're not close friends, but I know them well enough to invite them to a party. The biggest headache will be finding a heroine. She has to be pretty and she has to be able to sing."

"What's so difficult about that?" I asked. "Aren't there any pretty girls around?"

"Not many," Midge said, unwrapping a piece of gum and sticking it in her mouth. "But there are hundreds who think they are. And that's our problem. Every girl we ask will think she's ideal for the part."

"Why don't you play it?" I suggested.

"Don't be silly," Midge said. "I can't be assistant producer and your partner and have the most important part. The girls would all be mad at me before we started."

"They must get mad easily," I said.

"They do," Midge warned.

She finally came up with a list of seventeen to invite to the party. I knew only two of them and I didn't know them well. I met them for a few minutes last summer, according to Midge.

"You really ought to know something about each person—what he's good at or what he can do—so you can consider them for various parts while you are talking to them at the party," Midge suggested.

I agreed, and we decided that as soon as we had the time we would sit down and I would make notes while Midge told me about each one. First we had to decide on a date for the party and find out who could come. We finally picked Saturday evening. We are going to invite everyone for a cookout. We'll have hamburgers, hot dogs, potato chips, and corn on the cob. Uncle Al has a big vegetable garden this year and lots of corn that we can have.

Midge spent almost the whole afternoon on the telephone. When she decides to do something, she really works. By three o'clock we had fourteen who could come. She made a few substitutions because some of those she planned to ask weren't home. Aunt Mabel was going shopping so I went along to get the food and the soft drinks. Midge kept on telephoning.

Sunday, July 13th

It's raining today and there isn't anything I can do outside. I finished my book on fossils and I can't think of much to do inside either, so I might as well write a complete account of our party. I guess it was what the society editor of a newspaper would call "different."

Uncle Al had to go to Stroudsburg, Pennsylvania, on business on Friday. You go through the Delaware Water Gap to get there. That is where the Delaware River cuts through the Appalachian Mountains on its way to the sea.

"If you're interested in fossils and geology you ought to come along," Uncle Al suggested. "You will see all sorts of rock formations. Besides, it's beautiful country through there and the scenery alone is worth the ride."

Aunt Mabel decided to go and I asked Midge, thinking we could talk about who would be good for which part as we rode along. However, she had agreed to go riding with a friend during the afternoon and she has been to the Delaware Water Gap several times. We decided there would be plenty of time for a conference when I got back.

The trip was very interesting. I took my books on geology and fossils along. I didn't have a chance to hunt for fossils, but I did see several rock formations which fit the descriptions in my book. We were much later than we had expected in starting back, so we stopped to eat dinner on the way. It was after eight thirty when we got to Grover's Corner. I called Midge right away.

"Don't worry about a thing," Midge said. "While the great play producer and director has been enjoying himself sightseeing, his tireless staff has been hard at work. The information you need is all down on tape."

"What are you talking about?"

"Dad's tape recorder has been home for three or four days. It's a portable one that he takes to meetings and conferences. It uses little tape cassettes and is simple to operate. I had a brilliant idea. I dictated a complete character sketch of every person—name, description, what he's good at, what's wrong with him—everything. It's lots of fun to sit down and say exactly what you think about people, even if you're just talking to a tape recorder."

"How do I play it back? I don't have a tape recorder."

"You can borrow Dad's. If he should take it to the

office, you can play it back on our new AM/FM stereo set in the rumpus room. There's a slot for the cassettes. You just push one in and press the switch, and out come the unforgettable voices of stars like Janis Joplin and Midge Glass."

"Wonderful," I said. "I have to admit that I have a brilliant staff."

"I'm glad that you realize that," Midge said. "And I want to warn you that there's a lot more talent on your staff than in this bunch we've invited to the party. When I got down to bare facts about each person, it seemed to me that we're awfully short on brains and awfully long on creeps. I gave you my opinion on which part I thought each one might be best for, but I'm glad that you're the one who has to decide, not me. We haven't got what I would call an outstanding group. All I can say is that you'd better be a brilliant director or it won't be much of a play."

I decided that Midge was just feeling gloomy. At least we were getting a group together to talk about the play, which was more than I'd accomplished all summer, what with interruptions from Galileo.

I went over to Midge's Saturday morning to listen to the tape. Her father had taken the portable recorder to some meeting so I went down to their play room or rumpus room, whatever it is called, to listen to it there. Before I had figured out how to operate the equipment, Midge came in to tell me we didn't have any charcoal for the grill. I knew Uncle Al was going to Hopewell for something so I hurried home to go with him. I got the charcoal and some more Coca-Cola.

What with one thing and another, I never did get back to listen to the tape. We had the party in Midge's back yard. The grass needed mowing, and we had to get the grill ready, find some extra chairs, and do a dozen other things. I never realized before how much work it is to have a party. It was after four when we finished, and by that time I had to go home and change clothes. We expected people to arrive about five.

Everyone we invited came, but for some reason or other the party had no zip from the beginning. No one seemed much interested in talking to anyone else and they all sat around with long faces. Parties are peculiar. Since my father is in the diplomatic service, my mother has to give quite a few parties. She says they are like cheese soufflés. You follow the same recipe every time, but some are light and fluffy and delicious and others are flat and soggy. Well, our party was flat and soggy.

Midge introduced me to everyone and did her best to get the party going. After a while she disappeared for a few minutes.

"Mom says to feed them early," she whispered to me when she came back. "Maybe they'll act more like they're alive after they've been fed."

For the next forty-five minutes or so, I cooked hamburgers and hot dogs. At least they could eat. I thought we were going to run out of food. I was so busy cooking and Midge so busy serving soft drinks and other things that neither of us had a chance to eat anything until after all the hamburgers were gone. We had a hot dog each. Finally I got all our guests filled up and was cooking a second hot dog for myself when Midge stood on a chair and called for everyone's attention.

"I told all of you over the telephone that Henry plans to put on a play. He watched Mr. Seminoff, the movie director, make a film and he knows quite a bit about directing, He's got a good play written by a boy from Baltimore. It's about a musical group and is real cool. Henry would like to tell you about it. We invited all of you because we thought you are very talented and would be perfect for the various parts."

She said this with a perfectly straight face and she even sounded as though she believed what she was saying. I guess someone, somewhere, didn't, because suddenly there was a great clap of thunder and it started to pour. It had begun to cloud up during the late afternoon but we had been so busy that we hadn't paid much attention.

"Everyone go to the rumpus room," Midge shouted. "Right through that door over there and down three steps. Make yourselves at home. Henry and I will be down as soon as we get things cleared away here."

They all did exactly as she said. Not one stayed to help. It was lucky they had eaten so much because there wasn't too much left to clear away. Still there were dishes of potato chips, rolls, paper plates, napkins, and things like that. We worked fast and the job didn't take long but it was raining harder every minute. By the time we finished we were soaked. Midge went upstairs to change into dry clothes and I went on down to the basement.

Someone had been smart enough to carry a case of Coca-Cola along when they hurried inside. Everyone was having a drink, listening to the radio, and talking. There were even some signs the party might get off the ground. The Glasses' new AM/FM set is a very good one with speakers at two opposite corners. The music sounds as though the orchestra was in the room. Some boy was switching from station to station.

"Quit fiddling with it and stop somewhere," a girl named Sally complained. "You've gone by about six good numbers."

"Let me pick a program," Harold Oglesby said, walking toward the radio.

I was feeling clammy and uncomfortable. My shoes squished when I walked and my hair was dripping water down my neck.

"Midge is changing and will be down in a few minutes," I said. "I think I'll run home and put on some dry clothes myself."

I couldn't get much wetter so I walked down the road to our house. I changed clothes, dried my hair with a towel, and then got a mop and sopped up the water I had dripped on the kitchen floor and stairs. All this took quite a few minutes. I found an umbrella and a raincoat and went back to Midge's. It had almost stopped raining by this time. When I got inside there wasn't anyone there except Midge and Harold

Oglesby. Midge was very upset about something but Harold seemed to think whatever had happened was uproariously funny. He was rocking back and forth in a big chair, doubled up from laughing.

"It was an accident," he said when he finally stopped laughing. "Just a plain pure accident. If you both could have seen the expression on Sally Petrie's face!" He started laughing again.

"What happened?" I asked. "Where is everybody?"

"They've gone home. The play is off," Midge said, looking as though she was about to cry. "Everybody got insulted and went home in a huff. And it was all Harold's fault!"

"So help me, it was an accident," Harold said, wiping the tears from his eyes. "Someone turned on the radio. Sally complained about the station and I went over to change it. Then I saw that you have a tape cassette player, so I picked up a tape lying on the table and put it in. I turned the switch to 'Tape' and that did it!"

"Did what?" I asked.

"He played the tape that I dictated for you," Midge said. "I'm ruined for life. I think I'll move to Mexico."

Harold switched the set on, put the tape cassette back in, rewound it to the beginning and began to play it.

"Memo to Henry Reed, director extraordinary, from his assistant, Midge Glass, secretary extraordinary," Midge's voice said clearly. "This is a thumbnail sketch of the people we have invited to the party tomorrow and where I think each will fit in the play. No punches are pulled. I'm going to tell it like it is.

"First there is Eddie Dubrow. He's a big pudgy boy with a round face. I think you met him once before. He's a nice guy and will do anything for you. He gets along with everyone and if he says he'll be in your play he'll come to practice regularly."

Harold pushed the "Stop" button. "Eddie was pleased there for a minute," Harold explained to me. "Then the bomb dropped on him." He started the tape again.

"The main trouble with Eddie is that he's dumb," Midge's voice continued. "We can't give him much of a part because he'll never memorize the lines. You had better figure on him as a stage hand, but not much else. Next is Sally Petrie. She's a pretty girl with brown hair, about five feet five. You won't have any trouble spotting her because she thinks she is about the most beautiful creature that has ever walked the earth. She can undoubtedly act, because she is always putting on an act of some kind. She's no good for the heroine's part because she can't sing. She's always off key and she's just tone-deaf enough not to know it. Also the heroine is supposed to have a husky voice and Sally's is high and squeaky. She might be a good mother for the heroine. You know, the woman who is always complaining. Sally is good at that."

"That went over big," Harold said, stopping the tape. "Everybody liked it except Sally."

Midge groaned and Harold started the tape again.

"Barry Wechsler would probably be pretty good for the part of Albert if we can get him to do anything," the tape continued. "But he's lazy. I guess his mother spoiled him and he expects everyone to wait on him. He's a good drummer, though, almost as good as he thinks he is."

"Barry wasn't really sore," Harold said to me. "But Alice Winkler blew her stack. Let me see if I can find Alice for you."

"Don't bother," Midge said. "You can turn that thing off." She turned toward me. "Guess who is the only person I didn't say anything bad about?"

"Well, she told things exactly like they were," Harold said, sticking out his chest. "She has excellent taste and judgment. She says that I am the best guitarist around and have talent and poise."

"I'm sorry, Henry," Midge said. "It looks like we haven't got any cast at all."

"All you need is a different play," Harold said. "One with only one character, a talented young man with a guitar."

There was a paperback book on the table beside Midge. She picked it up and threw it at Harold. He ducked.

"I didn't finish what I was going to say on the tape about Harold," she said. "And that is that in addition to being impossible he's a mean low-down double-crossing rat and I hate him!"

Harold started laughing again. A minute later we heard a horn out front. "That must be my father. I am sorry, Midge. It really was an accident."

He left and Midge and I sat there without saying anything for several minutes. I suppose a great director like Mr. Seminoff would have thought of something to do, some way to get a cast in spite of our party. I couldn't even think of anything to say to Midge. I could tell from the way she stared at the floor that she felt very badly about what had happened.

"Would you like to hear the rest of it?" she asked finally.

"What for? And don't worry about the play. I don't think any of that gang could act any way except hungry."

"They really did eat, didn't they?" Midge asked. "Just think of all that good food and hard work wasted."

"Well, Uncle Al warned me when I first talked about a play that he thought I would find bugs and worms and animals more interesting and sensible than actors and actresses."

"Your Uncle Al is one of the world's smartest men," Midge said.

"Maybe I'll make a documentary movie instead," I said. "Of worms, for instance."

"That's not a bad idea," Midge said. She grinned and I knew she was feeling better. "You missed a great chance to make a real-life film tonight. If you could just have been here with a camera when they played that tape! I'd love to have seen their faces."

Saturday morning, July 19th

The last few days have been very quiet. I've given up the idea of producing a play so I've done just what I happened to feel like doing and I've relaxed. It's good to be free of worries and responsibilities. I wrapped up the play and sent it back to Aunt Helen in Baltimore. Thursday night I told Uncle Al what I had decided.

"Well, I didn't want to discourage you, but I've thought right along that producing a play would not be exactly what I would call a vacation. Of course, you are like your mother, and you aren't happy unless you are busy doing something. Now me, I can see quite a bit of merit in just sitting and contemplating now and then."

Several minutes later he looked up from his paper and said, "Well, doesn't that beat all? Here's your horoscope, Henry. 'Today is a day of important decision for you. You would be wise to abandon impractical plans. You will be much happier in enterprises that take you out-of-doors.' "

I thought he was making it up, but he showed me the paper. Of course horoscopes are silly, but they are sort of fun, like having your fortune told by a gypsy fortuneteller with a crystal ball. Anyhow, I was already following the advice, because I went riding Thursday afternoon.

Friday I went fossil hunting. Aunt Mabel went to some club luncheon in Princeton, and since I would have been home alone for lunch anyhow, I packed a lunch and made an all-day trip of it. I borrowed Uncle Al's binoculars and was hiking down the road past the ranch when Midge called me.

"Trish is coming over today to go riding with me," she announced.

"That's nice," I said. "I'm going fossil hunting."

"Couldn't you wait a little while?" she asked. "She's going to be here about ten and I'd like you to meet her."

"Why?" I asked. I remembered her saying that her friend Trish had a fancy riding costume and an expensive horse and was impossible. I couldn't see any reason to meet her.

"Well, she's really very nice and she has a beautiful horse."

"I'll take Galileo," I said. "Besides, today I'd rather look at fossils than either Trish or her horse."

"All right. I'll tell you the real reason," Midge said.

"I was hoping you'd be around when she came, to say a few things about Galileo. You know, how smart he is—things like that."

I knew what was bothering her. Trish was going to come all dressed up in a swanky riding habit with her horse curried and brushed as though they were about to appear in a fancy horse show. Midge didn't mind the fact that she would be wearing faded blue jeans. That's what she wanted to wear. But Galileo, with his shambling, ambling gait and his ears cocked every which way, looking like a scrawny scarecrow, was another matter. Midge didn't want anyone sneering at her horse. She wanted this girl to know that in spite of his looks, Galileo was a smart and unusual nag. And she was depending on me to get this idea across.

It was only nine o'clock and I didn't want to waste an hour waiting for Trish to appear. Besides, if she wore such a fancy riding costume she would probably take so much time getting ready that she would be late.

I had a good idea. "Look, why don't you ride over toward the radio tower, the same route we took that first day we went riding on the Gleasons' horses? You know, through that pasture and along the stream."

"That's a nice ride," Midge said. "But why?"

"I'm going to be over there hunting fossils. Before you come to the spot where that woman claimed she saw the bloody corpse, you'll see a cliff on the far side of the stream. I'll be there. Ford the stream and come over to where I am. After you cross the stream it's sort of boggy, but don't let that stop you. I went through with Galileo and he's a good mud horse."

"Just what is all this for?" Midge asked suspiciously.

"I've got a plan."

"Well, your plans are usually pretty good," Midge admitted. "Unless Trish has some particular place she wants to go, we'll be by there. We're going to take some sandwiches so maybe we'll eat lunch with you."

I put my knapsack on my back and then, as I started to walk away, I said as sort of an afterthought, "After you cross the stream and head toward the cliff, be sure you and Galileo are in the lead. Don't let Trish get ahead of you."

Midge didn't say anything but I could see that she was trying to figure this out. I went hiking down the road before she could ask any questions.

It was a long walk to the cliff, especially since I didn't go the way I had gone when I was riding Galileo. I didn't want to walk across that mud flat, so I crossed the stream much sooner. I had to circle several swampy areas but finally I got to the cliff with reasonably dry feet.

The cliff was made of a dark red shale. It was in layers that split apart easily like slate. According to my book on geology, a long long time ago layers of silt had been deposited by water and then pressure had made it into the shale. I thought some leaves or bugs or fish might have been caught in the process and I would find their fossils.

I arrived about ten forty-five and hunted until almost noon without finding anything I was certain was a fossil. I did find one piece of shale that looked as though it might have the print of a fern on it, but it was so faint that I wasn't sure. I climbed up and down the cliff several times, which wasn't easy. Aunt Mabel had given me a practically new clothesline which she hadn't used since getting her dryer. I had this along and it was a big help. I tied it to a tree at the top of the cliff and used it in climbing up and down. The cliff had all sorts of jagged spots where you could put your feet but sometimes these would crumble away. Several times the rope kept me from falling.

By noon I was starving. I decided that Midge wasn't coming and was climbing to the top of the cliff to get my lunch from my knapsack when I heard her calling in the distance. I shouted back, scrambled on to the top, and got out my binoculars. They were not very far away. Midge was in the lead with Galileo moving along with that peculiar half-walk, half-trot of his, looking around as though he was the rider and was just enjoying the scenery. A few feet behind was a second horse, and it had to move right along to keep up. However, it was a beautiful horse. It practically glistened. Both it and its rider looked as though they were ready to ride into the ring at Madison Square Garden. The girl was wearing light-tan riding breeches, polished brown riding boots, a white shirt, and an elegant green summer riding coat. To top it all she wore one of those little black hats with a tiny brim that they call a hunt cap. She looked very smart, and she knew how to ride.

She sat very straight in the saddle. She and her prancing sorrel horse made Midge in her faded blue jeans,
and Galileo, look like poor country cousins.

I shouted and waved my arms and a minute later
Midge saw me. She turned Galileo toward the stream.
I sat down on the edge of the cliff where I had a good
view. I focused my binoculars carefully and waited.
They forded the stream at about the same point that I
had the day I had been riding Galileo. Midge was
riding at a reasonably fast walk with Trish's horse
prancing along only a few feet behind. Suddenly, just
as I expected, they were in mud above the horses'
fetlocks. Galileo continued to plow along, completely
unconcerned. He pulled his big feet out of the mud
and plopped them down again as though he enjoyed it.
I saw Midge look around in surprise as though wondering if it had suddenly started to rain. Then she
looked down at her arms. No doubt she had a crop of
mud freckles.

I didn't waste much time looking at Midge. I shifted
my binoculars to Trish. Most of the mud Galileo was
kicking up into the air was falling behind him, and
that beautiful riding costume was suddenly covered
with spots. Trish was just the right distance away. She
looked amazed, and then suddenly she let out a
screech. I think she said, "I'm being covered with
mud!" but I can't be certain. They were still too far
away to hear their words exactly.

Some horses are frightened of mud. I knew Galileo
wasn't, but I half expected Trish's horse would balk

or try to turn around. I certainly never expected he would do what he did. He walked on for a few feet, stopped, and then suddenly went down on his knees and started to roll over on his side. Mr. Ainsworth told me later that some horses will do that in a stream. They feel like taking a bath. I guess Trish's horse felt like a mud bath. Her horse was down before Trish realized what was happening but she slid off as he started to roll. She glared at him in a rage and let go of the reins. She tried to hurry away a few steps so he wouldn't splatter mud on her, but she tripped and fell down. When she got to her feet her face was muddy, her clothes were muddy, and mud dripped from the brim of her hunt cap. Her riding crop was still in her hand and for a minute I thought she might use it on her horse. I don't think she knew whether to hit him or cry.

The horse made up her mind for her. He finished his half roll, got to his feet, and started trotting after Galileo. His reins were still over his neck, so at least there was no danger of his tripping on them. Trish shouted at him and then went slogging through the mud after him.

Midge reined in Galileo. Trish hurried as fast as she could through the soggy swamp and tried to catch her horse. He moved away a few feet. She tried again and he moved again. He didn't feel like being caught. I guess this was a habit of his because Trish said something to Midge and shook her fist in disgust at her horse. Midge took one foot out of the stirrup and offered to help Trish get up behind her. Trish shook her head. They were more than halfway to the cliff by then and they decided to come the rest of the way. Galileo started plowing along toward me, Trish's horse circled off to one side keeping an eye on Trish, and Trish brought up the rear, having to pull each foot out of the mud at every step. I put my binoculars away and scrambled down the cliff to meet them.

She was a good sport. Some girls would have been crying at this point. She was too mad.

"I'll try to catch him for you," I said as they got near. "What's his name?"

"Sultan," Trish said. "And don't waste your time. When he gets loose this way I never can catch him. Usually he runs straight home. I've had to walk several times."

"Galileo is pretty dependable that way," I said. "You can fall off him and he'll stand."

Sultan didn't show any signs of wanting to run home. Probably this was because Galileo was along. A horse usually won't run off and leave another horse. However, he didn't show any signs of wanting to be caught, either. Each time I walked in his direction, he circled away.

"Trish, this is Henry Reed. Henry, this is Trish."

"I'm not usually covered with mud," Trish said, trying to wipe some of the mud off her face with a tissue. "What a mess! I'll have to send everything I've got on to the cleaners. And what a fuss my grandmother will make."

Trish seemed to have dark-brown hair, but with all the mud I wasn't certain. She was bigger and taller than Midge and had brown eyes.

"If you stick close to the cliff for a little way, you can cross back to the stream on solid ground up near the road," I told Midge. "There's a nice gravelly place in the stream where the water isn't very deep. Trish could get cleaned up there. There are bushes all around to hide you from the road. She could even take off some of her clothes and wash them if she wants. In this sun they'll dry fast."

"That's not a bad idea," Midge agreed. "How about it, Trish?"

"I hate to go back home looking this way," Trish said. "My grandmother used to ride a lot when she was a girl, and she never believes anything is the fault of the horse. It's always me. She'll think I fell off."

"That can happen to the best of riders," I said. "Leave Galileo here and Sultan will stick around. I'll see if I can't catch him."

Midge looked over at my rope, which was hanging down the cliff. "Maybe you can rope him," she suggested.

"Maybe," I said, but I didn't think much of the idea. Every time I try to lasso anything the loop gets all snarled up and looks like a tangle even before I throw it. I have never figured out how cowboys do it.

Midge tied Galileo to a small sapling. She took their lunch, and she and Trish began walking along the base of the cliff toward the road. They came to some firmer ground and cut back toward the stream. They must have found a spot where they could cross the stream without getting their feet wet because several minutes later they disappeared from sight.

Sultan walked over to within a few feet of Galileo and stood there. I tried to sneak up very quietly, but when I got about five feet from him he trotted away. Twice I tried sneaking up on him, once using Galileo to hide me. Sultan was too wary. Finally I decided I couldn't lose anything by trying to lasso him. I went to the top of the cliff and untied the rope and came down again. I made a loop and tried to get it swinging around my head the way a cowboy does. Once I managed to get a round open loop, but when I threw I didn't come near Sultan. On the next two throws, the loop closed the minute I made the toss. I guess I am not a natural roping expert.

I could see I was never going to catch Sultan by roping him, so I sat down to eat my lunch and think things over. I didn't think Sultan was as smart as Galileo, but he was suspicious.

Sultan didn't care much for the soggy, muddy areas. There was a narrow strip of firm ground along the base of the cliff, wide in some spots and quite narrow in others. At one point this strip was only about five feet wide and a tree growing right at the foot of the cliff made it even narrower. I figured that if I took Galileo on beyond this point and tied him, Sultan would try to join him, and he would go along the narrow path if he could.

First I coiled my rope and put it up in the tree. The tree had several fairly low limbs and was easy to climb. Then I chased Sultan in the opposite direction for a short distance. I ran back and led Galileo to a new spot beyond the tree. Then, as quickly as I could, I got up in the tree and waited. I was very quiet and I had my rope all ready.

Sultan hesitated for a few minutes and then slowly started toward Galileo. He looked around, trying to spot me. Horses don't seem to look up in the air very much. Finally he decided it was safe and walked right beneath my tree. It was simple. I lowered my noose a couple of feet and he practically walked into it. I pulled it tight and I had him.

I untied Galileo, got my things together, climbed in the saddle and, leading Sultan, headed toward the spot where Midge and Trish had disappeared. When I got about halfway there, I called to Midge.

"I've got Sultan," I called. "Is it all right to come?"

Midge shouted for me to wait a few minutes, so I sat there and ate my second sandwich. Then, when she shouted that Trish was dressed, I rode on.

They had done a very good job. Trish had sponged off her riding breeches. They looked pretty soggy, but they didn't have any mud on them. I guess she must have taken off her shirt and washed it in the stream as I had with my clothes, because it was clean too and sort of damp. Her green riding coat had been washed and was hanging on a bush. They had their lunch spread out and were starting to eat.

"You did it!" Midge said when she saw the noose around Sultan's neck. "I didn't know you were a roping expert."

"Galileo is a good cow pony," I said. I wasn't going to say I had climbed a tree and had snared Sultan the way they snare rabbits. If Trish hadn't been there, I might have told Midge, but this way I made Galileo look good, which is what Midge wanted.

"That's terrific," Trish said. "Now I won't have to walk or ride double with Midge. What's more important, if Sultan had gone home by himself my grandmother would have been worried sick."

They had an extra sandwich, which I ate. Then they got on their horses and rode off. Midge offered to let me ride double on Galileo but I wanted to do some more fossil hunting. I finally got home about five without ever finding anything. I may not be so good at finding fossils, but I have a reputation now around Grover's Corner for being an expert roper.

Saturday evening, July 19th

Midge came over this morning, not long after I had finished writing in my journal about Trish's accident yesterday. She was bubbling over with excitement about something. I could tell she had an idea.

"Let's go down to the R & G Ranch," she said. "I've got an idea, and it's easier to explain it when you can look at things there."

"How did everything turn out with Trish?" I asked as we started toward the barn.

"Wonderful!" Midge said. "You know, she's a good egg and I like her."

"She took that mud bath pretty well," I agreed. "What does she think of Galileo now?"

"She thinks he's a wonderful horse even if he isn't any beauty," Midge said. "She would have traded

Sultan for him yesterday and thrown in her riding costume to boot. But I wouldn't trade Galileo for any horse in the world." She looked at me suspiciously. "Did you know her horse would roll in the mud when you told me to ride over there?"

"Of course not," I said. "I knew how Galileo would act because I rode through that mud flat. I thought her horse might act up a little. And I knew she would get splattered with mud if she was behind Galileo. You said that she put on such airs with her riding costume, I thought a little mud might be a good idea."

"I was wrong about her. She really isn't a snob at all," Midge said. "But anyhow, it worked out very well. We came back to my house and did some more washing and some ironing. That coat of hers is washable and it looked like new by the time she left. Her grandmother bought her that outfit and Trish didn't want to go back with it all messy."

We arrived at the barn. Galileo was at the far side of the pasture, reaching up to grab some leaves from a tree. There was beautiful grass all around him but he wasn't interested. We climbed up on the fence and sat on the top rail.

"Before I explain my idea, will you give me an honest answer to a question?" Midge asked. "Remember, we're partners."

"Cross my heart," I said. "Honest answers."

"When you told me where to ride with Trish you said, 'Before you come to the spot where the woman claimed she saw the bloody corpse,'" Midge said. "But

175

you weren't there when she pointed out the spot. So
how did you know? Later you told us where to go to
get some of that mud off Trish. It was the same spot.
There is something peculiar about all this. What is going on?"

By this time Midge knew I could ride so I didn't
see much point in not telling her the truth. "I was
leaning over to tie my shoelace while Ginger was

drinking in the stream. He moved suddenly. I fell on my nose and got a nosebleed."

I told her the whole story. She thought it was a big joke but we decided we wouldn't say anything to Officer Haywood since the case was closed anyhow.

"Now I'll tell you my idea," Midge said. "It came to me last night when I thought about the wonderful job you did in lassoing Sultan."

I had just got rid of one story and there I was about to be stuck with another. The next thing Midge would be asking me to show people how I could lasso a horse, when I couldn't lasso a post from ten feet away. I decided to get out of this trap, too, while I was confessing.

"I didn't actually lasso Sultan," I said. "I balanced on my stomach on the limb of a tree and snared him as he walked underneath."

"Oh," said Midge. She was disappointed.

"What difference does it make?" I asked.

She thought a minute. "Not really any difference. The Busby boys can both use a rope. I saw them once at a Western horse show. Besides, you'd be too busy to be the roping star anyhow."

"What are you talking about?" I asked.

"A rodeo," Midge said. "I let you down on the play that you wanted to produce. That tape really fixed things. But I don't think a play would have been too great anyhow. Last night I had this terrific idea. Why don't you put on a rodeo instead? There are dozens and dozens of kids around with horses, and I know quite a few of them. Trish knows the others, and she will help. We could put up bleachers over there at the back of the paddock. We could have a parade, some roping, fancy riding, things like that."

"Do you think we could get some steers or calves to rope?" I asked.

"We could go see Abe Kaufman," Midge said. "He's a stock dealer and a wonderful guy. I know he'd help us if he has any steers."

"We could probably draw quite a crowd," I said. "They don't have many rodeos around here."

"We'll bill it as 'Henry Reed's Great Rodeo,' " Midge said. "The wildest and woolliest rodeo ever to be held in the state of New Jersey."

The more I thought about it, the better I liked the idea. We're going to schedule it sometime in August. Midge and I are going to hitch Galileo to the buggy tomorrow and go touring around to line up participants. All we need to do is drive along the back roads looking for horses. Even that will be easy, because Galileo whinnies when you get within a quarter of a mile of another horse.

Sunday, August 10th

I haven't written in my journal for almost a month.
A lot has happened that I should have recorded, but
I've been so busy that I haven't had time to write. I
know now why producers like my friend Mr. Seminoff never find time to write about their early struggles. They are too busy struggling.

It has been a lot of work but next Saturday, August
16th, Midge and I are all set to put on the greatest
rodeo ever held in New Jersey and maybe the greatest
ever held east of the Mississippi. It will probably make
me famous. I wouldn't be surprised if I get offers from
other cities like Cheyenne, Wyoming, to help with
their rodeos.

Finding people who want to be in a show involving
horses has certainly been much easier than trying to

find actors for a play. In fact, we have been able to pick and choose. It is amazing how many horses there are around. Usually wherever you find a horse, you find someone near our age. Also, people with horses don't go away for the summer as much as people without horses. Getting someone who will take care of a horse while you're away isn't easy, and having a horse boarded is expensive. So people stay home, take care of their own horses, and go riding.

The first thing I did was to go to the library and read everything I could find on rodeos. The Western rodeos have rules for all their events, and judges and timers who watch everything. The cowboys get money and also points for winning an event. Then the cowboy who gets the most points at all the rodeos is the champion bronc rider, champion roper, and so on. Western rodeos all seem to have about the same events —bronco riding with a saddle on the bucking bronco, bareback bronco riding, calf roping, team roping, bull-dogging, and wild-bull riding. Between main events they often have exhibitions of trick riding and roping, and clowns who do all sorts of funny things on horse-back.

I made a list of all the events and a few notes about the rules. Then Midge and I harnessed Galileo to the buggy and set out to find out who wanted to be in our show. I didn't have very high hopes because when I looked at the list of events, I wasn't sure who could perform in them. It seemed to me that the only one we could be sure of was the clown act. At least I had some costumes that a clown could wear.

Locating boys and girls who were anxious to try anything wasn't much of a problem. The trouble was that we didn't have any broncos that we could depend upon to buck, or any wild and woolly bulls for cowboys to ride. Also we ran into a few problems with mothers. Billy Wilson's mother is a good example. Billy said he would like to try bronco riding and bull riding both, but Mrs. Wilson didn't agree.

"You'll do nothing of the kind," she said. "I went to a rodeo once in Tucson. I'm not going to have you gored to death by some wild bull."

I told her that I doubted if we would be able to find any very wild bulls around Grover's Corner and that most of the bulls in our area didn't even have any horns. This didn't change her mind in the slightest. She finally agreed that Billy could enter the roping events if we had any, but that was all. He had never tried to rope anything, but he said he would practice.

At the end of the first day we decided we were going at things backward. What we needed first was the bucking broncos and wild steers. The next morning we went over to see Mr. Kaufman, the animal dealer. He is a short, stocky man with a tanned, leathery face and eyes that crinkle at the corners. He was interested immediately in our idea of a rodeo.

"I think maybe I can help you," he said after we had explained our problem. "I've got a pony that bucks. That's why I haven't been able to sell him. He's not big—about the size of a small Welsh pony—but he's strong, and can carry a full-grown man. He's not in the same class as some of the outlaws out West, but he'll put on a good show. And if the rider gets thrown he hasn't so far to fall. I don't have any bulls and I doubt if any of the farmers around here would be willing to let their high-priced bulls be ridden in a rodeo. Besides, it would be too dangerous. I do have four steers that are about three-fourths grown. They would probably cause a little excitement if anyone tried to ride them."

Mr. Kaufman suggested that we get sheep for the roping acts, since there were more sheep around than calves. "Get some sheep that are almost full-grown," he advised. "They're usually scary and dumb and will run from a horse. Most of the small calves around here are dairy calves, and they are so placid and tame that you could walk up to them and tie a rope around their necks."

"What will you charge us for using your bucking pony and the four steers?" I asked.

"Nothing," Mr. Kaufman said. "I'd like to see a rodeo. I'll bring them over in my truck. But I would like to put up a sign saying that I have ponies for sale."

We thanked him and started to leave. We had turned around and were going out the driveway when he called to us.

"I've just thought of something," he said. "Go see a man named Gavin Oliver who lives near Sergeantsville. He has a burro that bucks, and he might have something else that would interest you too."

Sergeantsville is five or six miles from here but we had our lunch along. It was about two thirty when we located Mr. Oliver's place. We were only part way up the lane when we saw the other reason why Mr. Kaufman had sent us there. Two tiny donkeys were standing by the fence near the barn.

Mr. Oliver was home and he came out to see what we wanted. He was a thin little man with white hair. He told us later that he used to work in New York City but is retired and keeps some animals around for fun.

"They're Sardinian donkeys," he explained after we had told him who we were.

"Are they full-grown?" Midge asked. She put her hand to the fence and the nearest donkey nuzzled it.

"These two are about eight years old," Mr. Oliver said. "I guess they weigh between 350 and 400 pounds."

I thought Midge would go out of her mind. She crooned to those two little donkeys the way some people do to babies. Of course they were a lot more attractive and interesting than any baby I've ever seen. One is black and the other is what I suppose you would call a donkey gray. They stand only about thirty inches tall at the withers, not much bigger than a large dog. They have big gentle eyes and soft noses. Mr. Oliver has a brightly painted cart for one and a saddle for the other.

"A donkey that size shouldn't carry anyone much bigger than a small child," he explained. "But they can pull quite a load in the cart. They are very dependable and gentle and I can't imagine a safer pet for a child. Their dispositions are totally different from that of a Mexican burro. I have one of those too, but he's stubborn and ornery. I used to have a bigger cart for him, but one day he kicked it to pieces. And he refuses to be ridden."

"Mr. Kaufman said you have a burro that bucks," I said. "That's what we came to see you about."

"He bucks, and sometimes he will run very fast for a short distance and then stop. You usually go right on over his head."

We stayed for almost an hour. Mr. Oliver agreed to let us borrow the two Sardinian donkeys and the burro for our rodeo. We aren't certain how the donkeys will fit into our program but they will be a hit even if all they do is stand around. We agreed that we wouldn't let anyone ride either donkey unless Mr. Oliver approved.

"Abe Kaufman called before you came," he said. "He'll take the burro over, and the donkeys too, for that matter. Or you can come get them in a station wagon."

With a bucking pony, a burro that didn't want to be ridden, four calves, and two little donkeys, we knew we could really have a rodeo. The next day we went back to signing up people who wanted to be in our show.

The first place we went was to the Busbys'. The Busby brothers are older than most of us. They're sixteen and seventeen. They are big for their age, they're good riders, and they lived on a ranch for

184

several years. They can rope and they have seen a lot of rodeos. There's no doubt they will be the stars of our show. Some of the other boys have been practicing, though. Billy Wilson is almost as good with a rope. With another month or so of practice, I think some of those in our show could be competition in a rodeo out West.

In three days Midge and I located twenty-three participants, ranging in age from eight to seventeen. All of them were enthusiastic about the idea and most of them have been over several times in the past three weeks to help us get ready for the big day. Everybody has worked very hard, especially Trish and the Busby boys. Of course Midge and I have worked hardest of all, but after all we are running the show. Uncle Al says the boss always works the hardest in any organization.

We had a few fence posts and rails left from building our corral, so we built two temporary pens near the far end of the main corral. The posts aren't very strong and the rails aren't either, since they are all the discards from our fence building. However, we won't be penning up wild Brahma bulls and they should be strong enough. Besides, the pens are inside the main corral and even if an animal gets out it can't go anywhere in particular. We built a gate in each pen that can be swung open so the lamb or calf has to go down a long narrow passage or chute. We have a gate at the end of the chute which can be opened to let the animal out to be roped or ridden. The Busby boys designed the whole layout after ones they had seen in Texas.

We lined the four sides of the sheep pen with slatted snow fence because small sheep can sometimes go right between the rails of a post-and-rail fence. Once they are released from the chute into the main corral they might possibly get out, but we hope they will be roped first. If they get out we'll just have to catch them.

Midge is going to be the chief announcer, with Trish as her helper and as judge. We have built a scaffold near the barn with a judge's box or stand at the top where Midge and Trish will stand. We will run an electric extension cord under the road the way we did when the Willy Nillies had their concert. Mr. Glass has promised to borrow some public-address equipment from a friend and set it up for us. Midge will have a microphone just like a professional entertainer.

The biggest project of all was building seats for the audience. Finally Billy Wilson solved that problem. His uncle works for a big lumberyard, and he was able to borrow some heavy planks and some cinder blocks. We built three rows of seats just behind the back fence of the corral. As people come in, they buy a ticket at the barn, then go around the barn and to their seats.

We even remembered that we had to get a permit from the township to hold an entertainment event open to the public. Uncle Al took care of that for us.

Everything is all set for the rodeo this coming Saturday except a few little details. Most of this week Midge and I are going to drive around in the buggy with a big sign advertising the time and the place of the rodeo. Everyone is calling his friends, we've had an article in the Princeton *Bugle*, and Mr. Adams from the radio station has promised to announce it over the radio. I think we will have a good turnout if the weather is good.

Thursday, August 14th

We almost made a terrible mistake. We forgot all about the sheep for the roping events. Mr. Kaufman had suggested the sheep, but he didn't have any. Neither Midge nor I thought about it again because we have been so busy. Besides, Mr. Baines, who has the farm right behind Uncle Al's house, has a whole flock of sheep. He's very friendly and several times when his sheep have got out, Midge and I have helped him drive them back in. I suppose the reason we didn't worry was that we felt certain Mr. Baines would be able to help us.

Tuesday we realized suddenly that we had to do something. I tried calling Mr. Baines on the telephone several times, but there was no answer. Before dinner Tuesday night, I saw a car drive in Mr. Baines's lane, so I walked back to his house. Some man whom I didn't know was filling the watering troughs for the cattle. I talked to him and found out that Mr. and Mrs. Baines were away for two weeks on vacation. They were driving to Yellowstone National Park and back. The friend who was taking care of their place was very nice, but he said he couldn't give me permission to use Mr. Baines's sheep in a rodeo. If I had just gone to see Mr. Baines earlier I would have been all set.

Wednesday morning Midge and I set out to locate some sheep. We had our sign on the buggy, so we were able to do two things at once. We saw sheep at several places but we didn't know the owners. We asked two people anyhow, but they didn't think much of the idea of lending us sheep to be roped at a rodeo. One woman said they were about to have several of their lambs slaughtered for the freezer and she didn't want all the fat run off the lamb chops. By the middle of the afternoon we were getting worried. We came to a place on Cherry Hill Road which had a field with a pond and, beside the pond, a number of sheep. Midge didn't recognize the name on the mailbox but we drove in anyhow.

You couldn't see the house from the road. The lane twisted through a grove of pine trees and suddenly you were in the parking area. There was a small white house on one side and a pasture on the other. I didn't pay much attention to the house because I was too busy trying to figure out what the two crazy figures in the pasture were doing.

There were two ponies about a hundred feet apart. They were normal-looking ponies, a little fat perhaps, but otherwise not unusual. But I wasn't sure if the figures on their backs were human or not. They seemed to have heads, and on the heads were what looked like helmets. They were stocky, lumpy figures and they seemed to be wrapped in aluminum foil.

"What are they?" I asked.

"They look like baked potatoes," Midge said. "Only baked potatoes don't ride horses."

Each figure was carrying a long pole in his right hand and a round aluminum disc in his left. Suddenly one of them shouted, "Charge!" They lowered their poles, kicked their ponies in the flanks, and began trotting toward each other.

"They're knights!" I said. "It's a tournament."

Sure enough, they tried to knock each other off their horses. On the ends of their lances were pads instead of points. The round discs were shields. Both knights missed on the first try. On the second charge, one knocked the other off. They were riding bareback, and actually the boy wasn't knocked off but just pushed back until he slid off the rear end of his pony. He landed on his feet but immediately lay down and pretended to be unconscious. The winner jumped off his pony, produced a wooden sword from somewhere, and put the point of it against the fallen boy's chest.

"Spare him, Sir Launcelot!" Midge shouted.

The boy turned to look at us. "Sir Harold," he said.

They didn't seem at all surprised at seeing a horse

and buggy in their yard, but then I guess anyone who is in a tournament with lances, armor, and war horses wouldn't be much surprised at anything. Both boys came walking toward the fence, and Midge and I got out to meet them. They were about ten years old and they weren't nearly as stocky as they looked. They were well padded. They were wearing chest and leg protectors like those worn by catchers on baseball teams. Aluminum foil had been glued to the padding to make it look like metal. The lances were long poles with hand guards and big knobs on the ends. I felt one. It was sponge rubber covered with cloth. The shields were round pieces of plywood with a handgrip fastened on the back. They had been painted with aluminum paint. One had what looked like a lizard painted on it. It was meant to be a dragon. The other had a fierce-looking wolf. All their armor—lances, shields, swords, everything—was handmade except the helmets. I thought at first they were real metal helmets because they had visors that opened and closed. However, they were plastic. We found out later that an aunt had sent them as a present. The helmets were what had given them the idea of becoming knights.

"What's your name?" I asked the second boy, as he raised the visor of his helmet.

"Sir Gerald," he said.

"Sir Harold and Sir Gerald," Midge said. "That's nice. What are your real names?"

"Harold and Gerald Farrell," they said together. "We're twins."

191

Harold looked over at Galileo. "If you can ride that horse, I'll challenge you to a joust."

"I haven't got any armor," I said. "We came in to see if we could borrow some sheep."

"What for?" Gerald asked.

"We're having a rodeo," I explained, pointing to the sign on our buggy. "We need sheep for our roping events."

"We'd like to be in your rodeo," Harold said. Or maybe it was Gerald. I'm never certain who says what, with those two. "Could we be in it if we lent you some sheep?"

"If you can rope or ride a bucking bronco, or ride a steer, sure you can be in it," I said. "And even if you can't do any of those you can be in the big parades at the beginning and at the end."

"Why couldn't we have a tournament?" they asked.

"Why not?" Midge asked. "That would be different."

It would be different, all right—too different. Before I could think of some tactful way of telling them that a contest between two armored knights just wouldn't fit in a Western rodeo, they rushed off to ask their mother about the sheep.

"In case they come back and say we can borrow the sheep, we've got to talk them out of the idea of a tournament," I said to Midge. "Think of something they can do."

"Why?" Midge asked. "People might like it. It would add a little variety."

"We're running a rodeo, not a variety show," I said.

The boys were back in several minutes with their mother. She was a vague woman who didn't have much of an idea what a rodeo was. She seemed to feel it was just a horse show.

"You're welcome to use the sheep if you'll promise they won't be hurt," she said. "And I think it's just lovely that you've asked the boys to joust as part of your show. You've no idea how hard they've worked on their armor and equipment. They've read every book on knighthood they can get their hands on. They eat, sleep, and dream about being knights."

There didn't seem to be any way I could get out of having their jousting act unless I wanted to look for sheep someplace else. I did manage to convince them they shouldn't wear their armor for the big opening parade. I told them to save it for their act and it would be much more of a surprise. I still don't like the idea. A rodeo should be a rodeo, even in New Jersey.

Sunday, August 17th

We had our rodeo. It was a great success. Everybody liked it, and I think they got their money's worth. We had over a hundred people who bought tickets at a dollar a ticket. We paid all our expenses, gave some cash prizes for various events, and divided up what was left. We got about two dollars apiece, which isn't much, but all of us had a great time. Mr. Kaufman sold one pony.

All the acts went off fairly smoothly. Of course there were a few hitches, but then every show has a few things go wrong. We were lucky because the only trouble worth mentioning came at the very end of the rodeo when it didn't matter much. We had everything we planned to have, except the final parade. We canceled that.

We started out with the Grand Opening Parade. Everyone was in that except me. I ran our public-address system during the parade and told who everyone was. We brought over the Glasses' tape player from the rumpus room, but this time we made certain we had the right tape. We had a recording of a brass band playing a march. First in line was Midge driving Galileo hitched to the buggy. It carried a sign saying, *Welcome to Henry Reed's Great Rodeo*. Galileo loves any sort of parade and he pranced along enjoying the crowd. After the buggy came Trish riding her horse. Her grandmother had bought her a complete new Western costume for the rodeo and she had borrowed a Western saddle. Then came the two Busby boys, the Farrell twins without armor, and Billy Wilson on his horse. Behind Billy was one of the Sardinian donkeys hitched to its cart. Tied behind the cart was the Mexican burro, but no one was on him. When we practiced earlier he went along on a lead without any trouble, but during the parade he balked right in front of the stands. He wouldn't move and held up the whole parade until Mr. Glass climbed over the fence and swatted him on the rump. After the burro we had fourteen horses and riders. Then at the very last Millie Poloski rode the other little donkey. Millie is ten, but she is very small for her age. Midge arranged the order of the parade, and she put the two biggest horses just ahead of that tiny donkey. We gave Millie a little pennant on a stick which she carried. It said, *The End*.

Mr. Kaufman brought four extra ponies, which we

put in the pen with the calves with a sign that they were for sale. If we had known in time we might have found saddles and riders for them, too, but as it was the parade was very impressive.

As soon as the parade was over, Midge announced the first event, which was sheep roping. We had four contestants. Of course Dick and Herb Busby won first and second prizes. However, Billy Wilson roped two sheep on the first try each time. Even John Wiley finally roped one. We had twelve sheep and each of them was released and caught once. Sheep, especially young ones like these, are fast, and roping them is not easy.

After the roping competition, Millie put on a comedy roping act. We had a little wooden horse that rolled on wheels and we tied ropes to each end. Two boys pulled it back and forth and Millie on the Sardinian donkey pretended to rope it. She doesn't know how to use a lariat at all and she wasn't expected to rope anything. The funny thing is that by accident she did. The whole audience clapped and cheered.

The next event was riding calves, only we called it "Wild Bull Riding." Midge was a very good Master of Ceremonies and made funny remarks about each person and act. We expected the Busby boys to win again and Dick Busby was one of the winners. But Herb Busby's calf threw him. Then came the big surprise of the day. Jenny Lindgren, who is quite a tomboy, rode one steer and did a wonderful job. The crowd cheered and shouted and Trish gave her the first prize.

196

Al Swartz won third prize. He was thrown, but he stayed on longer than Herb Busby. Four other boys tried the event and we had to use each calf twice. However, the calves didn't get very tired, because most of the riders stayed on only a few seconds.

Trish put on a riding exhibition next, going over some hurdles and dodging some barrels that we put up as obstacles. She can ride very well, and her horse is well trained. I think she enjoyed putting on a solo act and the crowd enjoyed it too.

Next we had some trick riding by three boys who stood up in their saddles and did things like that. They were a lot better than I would have been, but they weren't expert. I guess this was our poorest act. The crowd was very polite, though, and clapped much harder and longer than I expected. Of course the riders may have had a lot of relatives in the stands.

The bronco riding was the last of the big events. Since we had only one pony and one burro for this event and nine boys who wanted to ride, we had only bareback riding and no first, second, or third prizes. Naturally the fourth or fifth rider had a big advantage over the first because the horse got tired. Everyone drew lots for his turn. Anyone who stayed on for thirty seconds got a prize. The pony put on quite a wild bucking act, but both the Busby boys and two other riders stayed on long enough to win. Herb Busby was the only one who stayed on the burro for thirty seconds. That burro was smart. He knew more tricks by far than the pony. He would pretend to stumble and then suddenly buck and twist at the same time. He dumped most of the riders by running halfway across the paddock and then bracing his feet and sliding to a sudden stop. The whole event was very exciting and the audience thought it was wonderful.

Sir Harold and Sir Gerald were the last act. They were to be just before the Grand Finale Parade. They put on their armor in the barn and waited for the signal to come out and surprise everyone. All the others who had finished had tied their horses to a rail outside the gate where they would be handy for the parade. Most of the riders went around to the stands to watch the great tournament. Midge and I had been very mysterious about it and they weren't certain what to expect.

The twelve sheep were in their pen, and the four calves, the bucking pony, the burro, and Mr. Kaufman's four extra ponies were in the other. The two Sardinian donkeys were outside near the gate, tied to a little bush. All the hurdles had been cleared away, the barrels for the obstacle race had been removed, and the entire paddock was empty and ready for the two knights. Midge and I had worked on her announcements for several days. This was her favorite.

"Ladies and gentlemen, our show has honored the great horsemen of Western America. The rodeo has recreated the action, the color, the courage of our great West. Now we would like to recreate the romance and excitement of another great age—this time of Western Europe, not America. We bring you the Age of Chivalry!"

Timmy Swartz, who is a bugler with the Boy Scouts, gave some impressive toots on his bugle. This was followed by some stirring music over the public-address system. Sir Harold and Sir Gerald rode out very solemnly. They made one circuit of the pasture and then took up positions at opposite ends of the field. Midge shut off the music.

"On our right we have Sir Harold," she announced. "He is the dauntless knight with the red dragon on his shield. He slew this fearsome dragon just outside Pennington, New Jersey. On our left is Sir Gerald, with the Wild Wolf of the Sourland Mountains on his shield. These two gallant knights will joust to the death or until one or the other cries for quarter. Are you ready? Chaaarge!"

Sir Harold and Sir Gerald kicked their ponies with their heels and went galloping toward each other. They really put some spirit in it. Harold missed completely, but Gerald's lance hit his brother in the shoulder. I thought the match was over. Both were riding bareback. Without stirrups it is difficult to get back erect once you've started to slide, but somehow Harold did it. The crowd roared.

They went back to their positions and waited for Midge's second signal. This time nothing much seemed to happen. Gerald missed entirely. Harold's lance hit his brother's and bounced up to bang against Gerald's helmet. They had agreed not to aim for the head because no one wants to be hit in the face, even with a blob of foam rubber. This wasn't much of a blow, but it broke one plastic hinge. When the visors were down, the boys looked through slots. The broken hinge made the visor drop down on one side, so that he could barely see.

He rode back to his station, put the end of his lance on the ground, and leaned the handle against his knee while he adjusted the visor so that he could see. When he was ready, he picked up his lance. He said something to Midge, who was in the stands almost above him.

"Charge!" she shouted.

Gerald started forward at a gallop, but Harold's pony began to act up and tried to go off to the right. By the time Harold got him straightened out, Gerald was almost to the center of the pasture. Then his visor slipped again and he couldn't see. He knew Harold was some distance away, so he kept on with his charge, trying to shove his visor up with the back of the hand that held his shield. I think he made it worse instead of better. Harold had a perfect chance to knock his brother off his horse, but he was a good sport and didn't try. Gerald charged right on past. The end of the lance was ahead of the pony by about six feet. The pony didn't swerve and the padded tip of the lance went *wham* against the fence post. The jolt pushed Gerald right off his horse. The pony turned and ran back in the other direction. If you think a knight with a lance doesn't pack a wallop, you're mistaken. Gerald snapped that post off right at the ground.

The fence wasn't completely down, and it would have been all right except for those crazy calves. They were scared out of their wits. I don't suppose I can blame them, seeing a knight in armor with a lance charging down on them. They raced around the pen like maniacs. One bumped against the broken post and that did it. The trouble was that the post was the corner one where the two pens joined. The twelve sheep, the four calves, and the ponies came charging out in one mad stampede. The burro ambled along after them. Gerald was still getting to his feet. With the visor down over his face, he didn't know how close he came to being run over by the charging herd.

Everything would still have been simple if it had not been for Galileo. He had been unhitched from the buggy and saddled for one of the boys to use for the roping event. He was tied to the hitching rail with the other horses. That was a mistake. I guess he got bored and untied himself. Instead of wandering away, he had come over to watch the excitement. This is the first time I've ever heard of a horse opening a gate to get back in a pasture, but that is what he did. He had opened the gate and was standing in the middle of the opening when the stampede started. One of the calves saw the opening and led the way. The whole mob went charging through before anyone could stop them. Three of the horses tethered outside were so excited that they broke loose and joined the runaways. The two little Sardinian donkeys pulled loose from the bush where they were tied and disappeared along with the others.

I don't know whether you would call a collection of

sheep, horses, calves, donkeys, and burros a herd, a
flock, or a mob, but whatever it was it went running
out onto the road. There was a screech of brakes and
then silence. Then the stands seemed to erupt and
people began running for the entrance, partly to see
what had happened and partly to help.

The stampede did not go far before it broke into
little pieces and scattered. By the time I got to the

road I saw only one horse in the distance, galloping down the highway. Two sheep were disappearing around the corner of Midge's house and the burro stood in the middle of the road, looking at a dark-green car and chewing on a mouthful of leaves. He was right in front of the car. It couldn't move and he didn't intend to. A tall, thin man got out and tried to shoo the burro off the road, but the burro didn't want to shoo. I looked again. The man was Officer Haywood, in civilian clothes. At this point Midge came running out. She had been up in the announcing stand and had had to climb down.

"It's my day off and I had no better sense than to drive near where you two live," Haywood said. "I should have my head examined."

We should have announced that we were going to have a great round-up instead of a final parade, but we didn't think of it in time. People began streaming out to their cars. All the traffic and noise didn't help much. Officer Haywood stayed until most of the cars had driven away and things had quieted down. Then we started after our escaped livestock. The whole gang who had been in the rodeo stayed to help.

Billy Wilson roped the burro and led it back to the pasture. Each of the Busby boys roped a calf. We were able to drive the other two back into the pasture. We got the missing ponies with a few lumps of sugar, and someone rode down the highway and caught the horse that had gone racing off. We couldn't locate either of the Sardinian donkeys for quite a while. We looked through everyone's yards and found six sheep, which we couldn't catch, but there was no sign of the donkeys.

"They must be at the Apples'," Midge said. "Something was bound to go there."

We found both the donkeys in the Apples' back yard. Mrs. Apple was feeding them apples. The donkey cart seemed to be in good condition and so were the donkeys.

"We had a stampede," I said. "I'm sorry they came over into your yard."

"They're darling," Mrs. Apple said. She was even pleasant. "If I had known you were going to have these at the rodeo, I would have gone."

Mr. Kaufman hauled away the calves and the ponies on his first trip. We tied up the burro and the donkeys and then opened the pasture gate. With at least twenty people helping, we rounded up the sheep and herded them back into the pasture. I had fixed up one of the small pens and we managed to get them into that. Everyone except Midge got on his horse and headed home. Midge and I waited for Mr. Kaufman to come back, and the three of us loaded the sheep, the burro and the donkeys. I went with Mr. Kaufman to deliver them and then he brought me home. It was after seven o'clock. The rodeo was over and I was tired and hungry. But it was a great show.

I don't think I'm going to be a producer after all. It's not that the rodeo wasn't a big success and a lot of fun. Uncle Al says it's a good idea to try different things so that you will learn what you really like. I learned one thing about show business, and that is that you should stick to one thing at a time. Never mix tournaments and rodeos, for example. I think I'll be a naturalist.

The MS READ-a-thon needs young readers!

Boys and girls between 6 and 14 can join the MS READ-a-thon and help find a cure for Multiple Sclerosis by reading books. And they get two rewards — the enjoyment of reading, and the great feeling that comes from helping others.

Parents and educators: For complete information call your local MS chapter, or call toll-free (800) 243-6000. Or mail the coupon below.

Kids can help, too!